BRING THE PAIN

BRING THE PAIN

THE UNBELIEVABLE MR. BROWNSTONE BOOK FOUR

MICHAEL ANDERLE

DISRUPTIVE IMAGINATION

BRING THE PAIN TEAM

Special Thanks
to Mike Ross
for BBQ Consulting
Jessie Rae's BBQ - Las Vegas, NV

Thanks to our Beta Reader
Natalie Roberts

Thanks to the JIT Readers

John Ashmore
Kelly O'Donnell
Dr. James Caplan
Peter Manis
Daniel Weigert
Paul Westman
Larry Omans
Micky Cocker

If I've missed anyone, please let me know!

Editor
Lynne Stiegler

*To Family, Friends and
Those Who Love
to Read.
May We All Enjoy Grace
to Live the Life We Are
Called.*

J ames grunted as he surveyed the two rental choices on the display in front of him, Toyota and Hyundai sedans.

The rental employee stood to the side, a smile stuck on her face. "Have you decided, sir? Both are excellent choices. Great mileage. Very comfortable."

"But no four-wheel drive?"

The woman looked confused for a moment. "You said you were interested in a family vehicle, sir, for a weekend trip to New York City, I believe?"

James did want a family vehicle. He wanted Alison to be comfortable on their weekend together, and it'd be easier for her with a vehicle lower to the ground, but the combat capabilities of his wheels never strayed far from his thoughts.

"I was thinking about maybe camping," the bounty hunter lied. "Smaller SUVs?"

I could take out the spare tire and stick some extra weapons in there. Alison wouldn't have to know about them, and it'd still be easy for her to get in and out.

James could see the annoyance dance in the woman's eyes, but she kept the plastic smile on her face. "We don't rent trucks here, sir, and all our SUVs have already been rented. I can offer you different choices if you want, but still in the same general class."

"Okay, I get it, I guess," he rumbled. "So that's a no on the four-wheel drive?"

"I'm sorry, sir. Neither vehicle has four-wheel drive. If I might say so, you really won't need that in New York City. I know they call it the concrete jungle sometimes, but it's not that bad." She chittered at her joke.

Things have been quiet. No reason to suspect anyone's coming after me or Alison, so probably shouldn't need to go off-road. But it wouldn't hurt if I need to lose some assholes.

James rubbed his chin as he thought that over. He resisted the urge to ask about how well either car could handle bullets or fireballs, even if the question rang in his mind. As long as he had good handling and speed he could avoid an RPG annihilating the car, but a rocket launcher might still prove too much. Then again, a rocket launcher would be too much for his F-350.

Someone needs to start a rental car business for people like me. Sometimes a family man needs to be able to kick ass and take a direct hit from a fucking rocket.

"Insurance," James blurted.

The rental employee blinked. "Excuse me, sir?"

"I want to take out the maximum in supplemental

insurance." James rubbed the back of his neck and tried to force a smile, but it came out a little more feral than he intended.

The woman gazed at him warily. "I...see. Do you have a problem with driving? Your license didn't have any points on it." Her tone dripped suspicion.

James wasn't about to admit that his clean driving record was because of his friendly connections with several police officers who were willing to overlook his traffic issues related to dealing with bounties and hitmen. Even though they'd fined him piles of money for his last adventure in LA, they hadn't put any points on his license.

The bounty hunter tried to think of a quick lie. "It's New York. They are terrible drivers there. Not that they are any better in LA." He shrugged. "You know assh...people in big cities."

The woman's face softened and she nodded in under-standing. "I suppose that's true enough. It's why I prefer Charlottesville. We're not a tiny town, but nor have we forgotten proper manners."

"Yeah, Alison's said that about the area—how nice everyone is compared to LA even if she doesn't get out much," James mumbled.

"Alison?"

"I'm picking her up from a local...prep school."

"Oh, I see. For your family weekend, I'm sure your daughter definitely would prefer a sedan."

James opened his mouth to correct the woman on Alison being his daughter but nodded instead. He might not have formally adopted her, but he also couldn't claim he hadn't started thinking of her that way. It was a strange feeling, both unsettling and comforting at the same time.

"Yeah, she's not big on the truck I drive back home." He frowned.

The bounty hunter's last adventure in renting a vehicle had ended with him having to pay for a completely new Humvee. Insurance had helped, but not enough to replace the entire vehicle. His quick payment had prevented any sort of lawsuit, though, or from what he could tell, any sort of black mark in the vehicle rental industry.

Need to stop thinking that just because I'm driving around, some asshole's gonna take a swing at me. No one's fucked with me on these weekends with Alison yet, anyway.

James' frown turned into a smile. Anyone who attacked him would probably be in a truck or SUV. He could always kill them and take their vehicle if necessary.

James nodded, satisfied with the plan. "I'll take the Toyota."

The Toyota would work. He'd shot up a lot of Toyotas in recent years. They didn't take a bullet like a Ford, but they were stubborn and persistent even with a few rounds in the engine block.

The rental employee shot him a bright smile. "An excellent choice, sir."

"It's got a spare tire, right?"

The woman looked insulted. "Of course, sir."

Not much room, but I can still hide a few .45s and 9mms with extra mags.

"Just don't want to get stranded, you know?"

"This vehicle has an excellent reliability record."

"Good to know."

They need to start including machine gun bursts when they test these cars.

James chuckled to himself, and the woman eyed him.

"Sorry, just thinking of a joke about New York."

James wanted his stay on the grounds of the School of Necessary Magic to be brief, so he didn't even get out of the car. He waited in the Toyota in the circle drive surrounding the phoenix fountain, glancing at the students walking around or waiting for their parents.

Every time he drove onto the school grounds his muscles tightened, and it was hard for the hair not to stand up on the back of his head. There was just too much magic in one spot for his taste here. When he was around Alison it was easy to concentrate on her and not let it get to him, but without her as an anchor he was forced to confront the reality of being in a place where normal people were in the minority.

Not that I'm fucking normal. Far from it.

James didn't hate magic. He used it on the job when needed, and he'd sent Alison to the school because he thought it would be the best way for her to learn about her abilities.

None of that changed the fact that a school filled with people who could do incredible things made him nervous. His abilities were impressive but straightforward. He wasn't shooting fireballs through holes in the air, changing his shape, or bringing dolls to life.

In the end, the bounty hunter distrusted magic because

it was a complicated tool rather than a simple solution like a nice punch or a bullet to the head.

He scanned the area, looking for any sign of the creature that had most unsettled him on his last few trips: the top-hat-wearing ferret. The fashionable rodent appeared absent, or at least he wasn't anywhere James could see him.

Probably getting a new fancy hat and spats. Pompous little prick.

James spotted Alison walking toward the circle drive and hurried out of the car to go help her with her bags.

The teen ambushed him with a hug and he hugged her back before pulling away.

"You sure you're okay with the drive up to New York?" James asked. "Long time in a car. We could always take a plane. It's not a big deal."

Alison tilted her head and smiled slightly. "But you don't *want* to take a plane."

James grunted. Acting as a parent for a girl who could see souls and could often tell if someone was lying could be difficult.

Talk about needing to have an open and clear relationship with your kid.

"I'm not crazy about flying, but I'll do it for you," he assured her.

The girl shook her head. "More time on the road just means more time to talk." She looked around for a moment with a confused look. "Aunt Shay isn't here?"

"She had some sh...stuff to take care of in LA for a job, but she's been to New York. She told me a ton of the best pizza places to try."

"Oh." Alison sighed. "Work is work." She eyed him. "You're not going to...work while you're there, right? This trip is just for us to hang out and not for you to find people to have *discussions* with?"

"Didn't have any plans to do anything but spend time with you."

"And you're not expecting any trouble?"

James chuckled. "I'm *always* expecting trouble, kid, but no one's told me anyone's after me. I think after my little meeting and *discussion* with the Harriken in LA that people have gotten the fu— They get that they should leave me alone. Sometimes it just takes a while to sink in."

Alison smiled. "Then it'll be a great weekend with just the two of us. I'm so excited." She bounced a little, looking very innocent and young for a girl who had suffered so much.

The smile warmed James' heart. Alison had been through a lot with the loss of her mother and her father's betrayal. She deserved to be happy.

The bounty hunter had never intended to acquire a family. If anything, he figured someone as fucked-up as him should stay far away from other people, but now it was hard to remember what it had been like before Alison. Colder. Emptier. Lonelier.

Even though she spent most of her time thousands of miles away from LA at the School of Necessary Magic, the fact that she was in his life gave him a reason to get up in the morning.

"Let's get to New York," James rumbled.

Alison had always wanted to see *Wicked*. The show had gone through a major revival because of its pro-witch and magical leanings. In addition, literary scholars had located notes indicating that the original Oz books had been influenced by encounters Baum had had with Oriceran visitors arriving via a strange tornado-gate spell. His plan had to have been to try and slowly spread awareness of the truth of magic in a way people might find acceptable, starting with children.

The teen didn't care much about the history. She just loved the idea of being surrounded by the music and the energy of the crowd.

When the actress playing Elphaba belted out the first lines of "Defying Gravity," the crowd roared in approval.

Alison sat back, enraptured. The singing was stunning and powerful, but not the true source of her enjoyment.

The instrumental accompaniment interlaced and supported the singing, as it would in any Broadway show, but the true glory was the bright colors of the souls of everyone in the room. It was as if the performance was tying them together into one giant entity awash in positive energy.

The swell of colors mirrored the pride and defiance of Elphaba as she sang about defying both gravity and the conventions of her society binding her. The bright colors in the crowd signaled their euphoria; the performance was overwhelming them.

The souls of the performers onstage shone even more brightly. A skilled actress might be able to fake a sighted person out with her performance. Alison couldn't see her face, but she could see the woman's lack of stress, fear, or nerves. The woman was enjoying herself, which made the girl love the song more.

Alison glanced at James. He was quiet, and his soul didn't shine with the euphoric happiness of almost everyone else. It kept its natural and constant beauty. He was also satisfied, more satisfied than she'd seen in a while.

Every note and every lyric rippled through the souls of the gathered crowd, the intensity and shades of their energy shifting in intensity with the song's emotions.

Alison had never witnessed over a thousand people united in feeling, even at her school during events. She'd never seen so many souls filled with joy.

The song finished and the crowd shot to their feet in a standing ovation as the curtain fell for the intermission. Their claps and cheers echoed in the theater. The excitement and happiness flowed together and for that brief, shining moment everyone became one.

In her short life the girl had dealt with both beauty and darkness in small groups, always believing the world was good at its core even after the horrible death of her mother. The show provided proof—the kind of evidence only she could see—of how beautiful the world could be when people let their souls shift away from darkness, if only for a short while.

Tears leaked from Alison's eyes. As she blinked the tears away she felt someone grab her hand.

The teen realized it was James. Streaks of the color of worry shot through his soul.

"You okay, kid?" James asked. "Is it too loud or something? Did someone say something?" A hint of menace entered his voice. "I'll make them regret it."

Alison shook her head. "I'm not sad. I'm happy. Just, everything's so beautiful. I love it."

"Huh. It's pretty nice, I guess. Maybe I'm just not enough of a musical guy to get all the details."

Alison laughed, not bothering to explain. "Thanks, James. I'm so happy you brought me here. I kind of feel like this show is about you."

"Me? How do you figure? I wasn't a nerdy green Witch last time I checked."

"No, but you're misunderstood, just like Elphaba. They called her the Wicked Witch of the West, but she was really just trying to protect and help the people she cared about and fight bad guys. Just like you."

James grunted. "I'm doing okay. The people who don't understand me don't mess with me. Maybe Elphaba should have lowered the boom from the beginning. Last few wizards who tried to harass me didn't like what happened to them." He frowned. "So, wait, if I'm the Wicked Witch of the West, does that make Shay the Wicked Witch of the East?"

Alison giggled. "Maybe."

"Better tell her to be careful about houses landing on her piloted by little punk girls from Kansas."

Alison laughed. "There's also a girl like Glinda at my school."

"A prissy two-faced bit— Um, a mean girl?"

"Yeah."

James frowned. "She's not pushing you around, is she?"

"No, I think she's like you—misunderstood."

"Guess you'd know better than I would."

Alison leaned over and gave James a squeeze. "Just remember that I will always believe in you, James."

2

The global head of the Harriken sat in the lone chair, surveying the gathered leaders kneeling at the table in the center of the room. There was a small box in his lap.

The failure of the subordinate was the failure of the leader. That principle defined the Harriken. The leader had earned the title of "Grandfather" for his cunning and strength, but that just left him as the person ultimately responsible for the failures of the entire group.

I should have executed Ikeda when I had the chance. Now I have inherited his shame, but at least in death he proved that even the great James Brownstone is a mere man, not a god.

Grandfather smiled to himself, remembering a few brief seconds of recovered footage that showed an enchanted *Masamune* sword piercing the bounty hunter. If Ikeda hadn't been an overconfident fool, he could have finished the man off right then and there.

Luck was a lie. Destiny, a joke. There were only opportunities and those smart enough to seize them.

"It is rare that I have you gather in Tokyo, even rarer that we gather in Tokyo twice in such a short period," the man began, glancing at his kneeling subordinates. "That I would have all my most trusted leaders gather here again is an inconvenience, but extraordinary times call for such measures." He waited for several seconds as everyone stared at him. "I assume most of you already know that Jiro Ikeda is dead at the hands of James Brownstone." He sneered.

Grandfather lifted the box and tossed it onto the table. The collision knocked the lid off and the contents spilled onto the table: Ikeda's rotting and severed left hand.

The gathered men murmured at the sight.

"Ikeda lost his hand for his failure, although he kept it as a reminder to do better, but this arrogant foreigner Brownstone sought to intimidate the Harriken by sending it to me. It's no matter. Most of the Harriken in America are now dead. What took our group twenty years to accomplish Brownstone has unraveled in months because of the uselessness of Ikeda and his underlings. People mock us on the internet and praise Brownstone as 'the Scourge of Harriken.'" He clenched his fist. "Unacceptable. Completely unacceptable."

Several of the other leaders exchanged glances, but no one said anything.

Grandfather took a deep breath and slowly let it out. "But this is my failure as well. I should have replaced Ikeda when I had the chance, so now I will take personal responsibility for controlling this matter. I will show the world why the Harriken should be feared." He stood, voice rising. "Those who think now that they don't have to obey us because of Brownstone will have nightmares about our might. We will reassert ourselves and destroy any who dare threaten us. We are the *Harriken*. We fear nothing, and all fear us!"

Several of the men cheered and others gave him uneasy looks.

Grandfather sat again with a smirk of confidence. He knew what they were thinking. Some were probably already planning to oust him from his position should he fail—as well they should. The Harriken had no place for the incompetent. Strength demanded respect. Weakness should and would be purged.

"I will personally see to the destruction of James Brownstone. I will ensure that he's captured, and I guarantee he will he suffer torments previously delivered only by angry gods and monsters. When I'm done I will take his head, stuff it, and put it on this table as a reminder of what happens to those who oppose the Harriken."

Enjoy your last few weeks on this planet, James Brownstone.

———

James wasn't all that much for musicals, but he did like seeing Alison happy. Because she was enjoying it the show didn't feel painfully long to him, even if his mind kept drifting off to thoughts of pizza and barbecue. The bounty hunter and the girl filed out of the theater after most of the crowd had left, James keeping a protective arm around her.

Even though he knew her soul sight let her navigate around people and animals with ease, it was hard for him to ignore the fact that she was technically blind. He wanted to do everything he could to make her more comfortable.

Alison spent most of the walk back to the densely-packed parking garage and the rented Toyota talking about her favorite songs from the show and the reaction of the crowd to the play. James offered the occasional nod or grunt in response.

After they arrived at the car, James did a quick inspection for anything suspicious. He wasn't sure if Alison would pick up on his worries with her soul-sight, so he started from the passenger side and worked his way around the back so it'd look like he was just going the long way to his seat.

Yeah, she's probably seeing right through this shit, but at least she's not saying anything.

When James finally slipped into the driver's seat, he couldn't help but chuckle at the girl's comparison of him to the misunderstood Elphaba. Other than the occasional concern about AET getting a little trigger-happy, James had never felt that he was misunderstood.

He wanted people to know that he was a tough bounty hunter, and that's what most of them believed. He didn't lie awake at night worrying about people thinking he was an asshole.

"What's so funny?" Alison asked as he tugged on her seatbelt.

"You comparing me to the Wicked Witch of the West earlier. It's kind of a strange comparison."

"Are you mad?"

"No, no. It's just, I'm not sure it fits."

Alison looked down. "I meant it in a good way."

"Yeah, I know. Don't worry about it, kid. Like I said, I'm not mad. It's funny, is all."

James pulled out of the parking spot, drove to the parking gate, and waved his phone over the payment sensor. The bar rose, and he pulled into the busy street.

Alison let out a long sigh. "I...do have a question. Something I've wanted to ask you for a while."

James grimaced. He hoped she wasn't going to ask him about sex. There were some conversations he wasn't ready to have yet.

"Go ahead and ask."

"In the show," Alison began, "you know, Elphaba gets mad, and with a lot of the stuff she does she isn't sure if she's doing it because it's the right thing, or because she's just kind of freaking out and reacting."

James grunted. "Yeah, that's pretty much life for a lot of people, whether they are Witches in Oz or guys working in an office."

"I see. Do you like your job?"

The bounty hunter spared Alison a glance, surprised at the apparent non-sequitur. "Huh?"

"Your bounty-hunting job. Do you like it?"

As James thought the question over, the muscles in his shoulders and neck tightened. This was dangerous territory on the best of days.

"I don't know how to answer that. I'm not gonna lie. I like a good fight, and when I take down a bad guy I feel satisfied. It's not always fun or whatever, though. A lot of days the jobs can be annoying, and some of these guys are such scum it turns my stomach."

"Why do you do it, then? I know how much money you have."

James shrugged. "I guess I do it because someone has to." He frowned. "There's other stuff, too, but I don't want to talk about that."

Alison gave a slight nod and turned toward the window.

James didn't want to hurt the girl's feelings, but he wasn't prepared to talk about the lingering pain of the death of Father Thomas. At times, James wondered if he could have saved the man if he'd had access to the amulet.

James sighed. "Look, kid, if there's something on your mind, just talk to me. I didn't want you to shut up. I've just got a shi...lot of issues I'm still working through, and I'm not a great guy to talk to about my feelings."

"I guess I was just curious about if you ever get angry at people when you do your job."

"That's an easy one. Sure. Most of the people I go after are complete pieces of garbage, Alison. They've hurt a lot of innocent people, so yeah, I get angry a lot when I'm on the job, especially when they won't come along quietly or hurt other people when I'm going after them."

James changed lanes, glancing at a stream of drones passing overhead. The greater population of NYC was packed into a small area, especially in Manhattan, which led to more people, cars, and drones than James was used to. The drones formed a river of buzzing metal and plastic in the sky.

"When you get angry," Alison asked quietly, "do you want to hurt people?"

"Not always, but..." The bounty hunter sucked in a

breath. Even if the girl could see into his soul, he didn't like the idea of voicing the words.

"But what?"

James grunted. "You know why I originally went after the Harriken, right?"

"Because they killed Leeroy?"

"Yeah. If people hurt someone I love or even threaten to hurt someone I love, I get fucking angry. Real fucking angry." James didn't even bother to try and hold back the cursing this time or control the angry quake in his voice. "I've lost too much family already, so I cherish what little I have. Any asshole who threatens that... Well, they get what they have coming. Live by the sword, die by the sword, as Father McCartney might say."

"What if someone did something bad by accident?"

James shook his head. "That's different, but it hasn't come up yet."

Alison didn't say anything, and James wondered if he'd scared the girl with his intensity.

Fuck. This is why I didn't want to talk about any of this. She doesn't need my shit weighing her down.

They'd driven in silence for a good five minutes before the teen spoke again.

"Have you ever thought about doing a different job?"

"Why? You worried about me?"

"A little, but...it's not that."

"What is it then?"

Alison looked at him for a moment, her eyes unfocused as always. "Your soul doesn't match the angry bounty hunter. It's...beautiful. It's like you were meant for something else."

James chuckled. "I don't know, kid. You probably know better than anyone but God what my soul is like. When I was younger I thought about being a priest for a little bit, but I think it's good I never decided to become one. I don't have the patience." He snorted. "I don't know how my confessor puts up with me half the time."

"I don't know a lot about priests, but I think you would have made a good one. Maybe you would have scared people into behaving."

"That's one way to do it."

James pulled the Toyota into a McDonald's parking lot. "Figured we could get a little snack before we continue with our sightseeing. McDonald's okay?"

"Yeah, sure." The girl's voice sounded distant.

The bounty hunter parked between an Audi and a newer-model Ford truck and forced down the grunt that wanted to rise. He missed his F-350.

"You killed that King Pyro guy," Alison continued, looking away.

James' stomach tightened. "Yeah, I did."

"Did he say something about hurting people you love?"

"Yeah, he did." James turned to look directly at the girl. "He had killed innocent people before so I had no problem wanting to take him down, but then he bragged about how he was going to go after the people I cared about. Even though you were safe, I got really angry at the idea that he might go after you, so I finished him off." He gritted his teeth and sucked in a breath. "And no, I don't regret it."

Alison fingered her necklace, a jeweled pendant on a silver chain. James' gift was fashionable enough, but the real power was in its defensive magic. It was another small way he could protect her even when he was far away.

Tears slipped down her cheeks, and her sniffles soon grew into full-blown sobs.

Oh, shit. Did I scare her? What should I say?

"Uh…" was the best James could muster. "I'm sorry, kid."

Fuck. I wish Shay was here. She would know what to do.

Alison only cried louder.

James pulled his phone out of his jacket pocket and placed a video call to Shay. He muted the sound and waited for the call to connect.

The dark-haired field archaeologist answered with an annoyed look on her face. He turned the phone so Shay could see Alison and back, then shrugged.

Shay rolled her eyes and shook her head. She mimed placing the phone to her ear and waited.

James unmuted the phone and brought his phone to his ear.

"I don't know what you did to make her cry, but console her, you idiot," Shay hissed over the line. "Even if you think you didn't do anything, just…make the damned effort, okay? Hug her at least."

James grunted as he ended the call, then tossed the phone on the dashboard.

What if I just make her more pissed? Fuck.

A deep, slow breath followed, and the man reached over as if he were about to grab an unstable nuclear bomb. He unbuckled Alison's seat belt, pulled her into a gentle embrace, and patted her back.

The teen didn't jerk back, slap him, or spit in his face.

She buried her head on his shoulder, although she kept crying.

James didn't understand why she'd started crying or if it was his fault, but it didn't matter. He was the closest thing the girl had to a father now, and he needed to do what he could.

3

Alison calmed down after five more minutes, not offering any explanation for her emotional outburst. James was fine with not prodding the girl. Women's emotions usually confused him, let alone a teen girl who had lost her parents and was still dealing with learning she possessed magical abilities.

James decided to go to a slightly more upscale place than McDonald's. Some fries and a salad later, Alison seemed more relaxed. They didn't talk much, though.

The girl didn't smile until they grabbed some ice cream. They strolled down the street side-by-side after that.

Even though the sun had long since set, the light poles, along with the haze of light suffusing the city, prevented true darkness.

"I'm sorry," Alison blurted.

"For what?" James asked.

"For freaking out. I guess..." Alison shook her head. "Sometimes I feel helpless and I worry about you, is all."

"You're not helpless, kid. You've got *powerful* magic, from what your teachers keep telling you. It'll come soon enough, and then you'll never have to worry about anyone ever again."

Given what he'd seen in the aftermath of Alison's mother's magic, if the girl had half her power she would be a living WMD. The School of Necessary Magic would give her the discipline and training she needed to wield it safely.

The bounty hunter took several more steps before he realized Alison wasn't beside him. James' stomach tightened and he spun. Alison was a few yards behind him, staring across the street.

He glanced in the direction she was looking. Other than a few guys entering a bank, he didn't see anything interesting. Their coats were a bit heavy for the weather, but maybe New Yorkers were softer about temperatures than people from Los Angeles.

"What's up?" James asked, stepping toward her.

"Those three men…" Alison gestured toward the bank. "They're planning something bad. I can see the evil streaks in their souls."

The bounty hunter's face tightened. He didn't need a fancy degree in psychology to figure out what three men with evil intent might be planning in a bank, but it also wasn't his business.

Keep it simple, stupid. He lived his life using that philosophy, and part of keeping it simple was going only after people who threatened him, those he cared about, or bounties. Being a hero was a good way to make trouble for himself down the line.

The girl nodded toward the bank. "You can stop them, James. They might hurt people."

James gritted his teeth. He was carrying his .45 in a shoulder holster. If the bank robbers weren't enhanced criminals he could probably take them out without even using his gun, but leaving Alison alone on a New York street didn't sit well.

"We should just call the cops. They might not even have bounties."

Alison shook her head and crossed her arms. "No" didn't seem to be an acceptable answer.

"I can't just leave you here to go play hero," James added. "You're the most important thing for me to protect."

Alison laughed. "You remember how we met? The neighborhood I was walking around in when I found Leeroy is much rougher than this place. Don't worry. I've learned a few things. I'll be okay." Her smile disappeared. "Besides, I want to be nearby when you kick some butt for once. Maybe I won't feel as helpless then. And if you wait for the cops, it might be too late. I'll call them, but please go in there and stop them before someone gets hurt."

James shrugged and sighed.

Guess it's time to stop a bank robbery. Okay, so my special father/daughter time is gonna involve me kicking bank robbers' asses. Didn't see that coming.

"Don't worry, Alison." The bounty hunter cracked his knuckles. "Someone's gonna get hurt. It's just not gonna be anyone innocent."

James waited for a break in the traffic, then darted across the street. That didn't save him from getting a few loud honks.

"Fucking drunk-ass idiot!" a man yelled as he zoomed past.

Ignoring the angry drivers, the bounty hunter pushed into the bank just in time to see the three men yank pistols from their coats. One fired into the air, and several people shouted or screamed. The other two swept the room on either side, guns at the ready.

The lone security guard raised his hands. One of the robbers rushed over to him and yanked his gun out of his holster before pistol-whipping the man with his own weapon. The guard crumpled to the ground with a groan.

That was a dick move. I think I'm gonna enjoy beating you assholes down.

"Everyone down. After that, if anyone moves," the first man said, a rusty-haired man with an offset nose, "they fucking die."

Nose been broken a couple of times, asshole? I'm seeing another break in your near future. Not your lucky day.

The gathered crowd all dropped to the floor, several whimpering. James remained standing, but apparently they hadn't seen him since they didn't do anything.

Redhead grinned and gestured with his gun toward the cashier, a tiny pale woman. He reached with his free hand into his pocket and pulled out a small black cube. "Log into your account and connect this to your terminal. It'll do everything else, sweetheart. Easy as shit. You just have to stand there."

James snorted. He'd read about this sort of thing but had never seen it firsthand before. This was another problem with all the fancy technology in the world. It made protecting yourself harder, and in some cases made crime simpler and less risky. The assholes didn't even have to go into the vault.

Lazy-ass criminals. At least King Pyro actually melted his way into vaults.

James grunted. It was time to end this little game. The bounty hunter took several steps forward.

One of the men pointed his gun at James. "Didn't you hear my boy, you ugly sonofabitch? I'm being nice already by not shooting you for not hitting the floor, but you look a little stupid so I'm trying to be nice here."

"I'm gonna give you one chance to surrender," the bounty hunter rumbled. "After that, if you end up dead it's on you, fucker."

"Get a load of Mr. Hero here. Doesn't even have a gun. You know what, asshole? I'm gonna give you five seconds to get on your knees and beg me to not—"

James cut the man off with a fist to the face and the robber flew backward. The bounty hunter didn't wait for the man to hit the ground before he charged the second-closest robber.

The criminal had just enough time to rip his gaze from his falling friend and squeeze off a single round. The bullet whizzed by James' head and the heat and air displacement tickled his ear.

Yeah, that could have hurt.

The bounty hunter reached the second robber and bent his arm backward until it snapped with a loud crack. The man screamed and James knocked him out with a headbutt.

The man dropped and his gun clattered when it hit the tile floor.

"Geeze, this is almost too easy!" James laughed. He spent most days going after level-three or higher bounties, and recent weeks had been filled with assaults on Harriken strongholds or magical foes. Taking down three standard-issue bank robbers was barely a workout. He almost felt sorry for the little shits.

Redhead fired several rounds but James zigzagged, avoiding the bullets until he could slide behind the counter.

Okay, one round at the beginning, three just then. That's four.

"You fucking piece of shit," the robber yelled. "No one had to get hurt, but now I'm gonna enjoy seeing you bleed."

"It's good to have dreams, asshole. Just remember that most people never achieve their dreams."

"I'm going to fucking bleed you out shot by shot, you cocky sonofabitch."

James' hand went to his .45, but he shook his head and slowly let his hand drop to his side. If they started trading much lead, someone who didn't have it coming might get hurt.

Shit. This is why I don't like playing hero. It's never fucking simple.

"Give it up, asshole," James shouted back. "Even if you get away, your buddies there will give you up to the cops. Just surrender. It'll go easier for everyone, especially you. You keep this shit up you're gonna end up dead, or at least busted up and even uglier than you already are."

"Fuck you, prick." Several bullets ripped through the wood of the counter in front of James. "You ain't shit."

Five, six, seven.

James shook his head. *Nobody ever takes the easy way out.* He looked at several desks lining the side of the room next to him and sprinted toward the nearest, then slid behind it.

Redhead squeezed off more shots, but he couldn't hit the fast-moving bounty hunter.

Eight, nine, ten, eleven.

The robber continued firing, perforating the desk, the computer monitor, and shattering some poor bank employee's mug that read **I Hate Mondays**. A few shards of ceramic landed on James' head.

Twelve, thirteen, fourteen, fifteen.

"You fucking get out right now," Redhead yelled, "or I'll put a bullet in one of these bitches."

James didn't get a great look at the man's gun, but the fact that he was now throwing out threats and not firing suggested one strong possibility: the bastard was out of ammo. The bounty hunter didn't remember seeing anything that looked like an extended magazine.

He grabbed the comfortable-looking chair behind the desk and, jerking upright, threw it straight toward the robber.

Sorry to whoever rides this desk normally. Now you're gonna hate Saturdays too.

The criminal's eyes widened and he turned to run, but the chair smacked into him and sent him sprawling. James leapt over the desk and sprinted toward the criminal.

When Redhead pushed the chair off him there was

MICHAEL ANDERLE

blood trickling down his forehead from a cut. His hand went to his gun just as the bounty hunter's booted foot landed. His yelp was cut off as James punted him with his other foot. The robber smashed into the counter a few yards away, embedded in the cracked wood. He groaned before falling unconscious.

James sighed and reached down to pick up the robber's gun. He strolled toward the robber, aimed at the man's leg, and pulled the trigger.

Click.

"Yeah, thought you were out." The bounty hunter smirked. "Next time bring some extra ammo, asshole." He tossed the gun to the ground. "If you're gonna be a criminal, at least put some professionalism into it."

James frowned as he spotted Alison hiding behind a potted ficus on the other side of the room—or trying to hide, at least.

Several NYPD officers rushed through the front door, guns drawn.

"Hands up. On the ground, asshole!" one of the officers shouted.

James grunted. At least it wasn't a trigger-happy AET team. He dropped to his knees and put his hands behind his neck.

"I'm not the robber," he told them. "The assholes I knocked out were."

"Shut your mouth," the cop yelled. He kept his weapon trained on James and another moved to cuff him.

It's just like the witch sang in Wicked. No good deed goes unpunished. Maybe I really am a misunderstood green nerdy Witch.

James chuckled.

"What's so funny, asshole?" the cop cuffing him asked. "You think twenty years in prison will be fucking funny?" He reached underneath James' jacket and pulled out his .45. "Oh, I bet a fucker like you doesn't have a permit for this bad boy. Maybe it's our lucky day and it's also stolen."

"You're making a mistake. I'm a bounty hunter."

"Didn't hear about any bounty on these guys. Everyone knows bounty hunters don't do shit without money involved."

Several more cops surged into the bank, guns drawn, and spread out like an angry swarm. Several pairs ran toward the hallways leading to the bathroom and the back.

"He stopped them," a timid female voice interjected into the din.

James glanced toward the voice. It was the cashier.

"Ma'am?" the cop asked. "What are you saying?"

"That man...with the tattoos and the weird face." The cashier gasped and put a hand over her mouth before giving James an apologetic look. "Sorry."

James grunted. "Not news that I have a strange face."

"He confronted the robbers. Told them to stop. They refused, so...he beat them up."

"Wait," another of the cops exclaimed, stepping toward James and looking him up and down. "I know this guy."

The cop with a weapon on him sneered. "Bounty on him?"

The other cop laughed. "Hell, no. He's James Brownstone. Licensed class-six bounty hunter. He's the guy they paid out to for taking down every Harriken in LA by his damned self."

James shrugged. "I had some help on the first batch. Friend of mine."

The cop who cuffed him pulled out James' wallet and flipped it open. "Yeah, looks like it."

"Uncuff me now, please?"

The two cops closest to him exchanged angry glances, but the first nodded to his partner and uncuffed James, handing his gun back.

"Thanks." James looked at the three unconscious robbers, now all flat on their backs and cuffed. "So, no bounties on those assholes?"

It wouldn't hurt to try and squeeze a little money out of the situation.

"Nah, these are some local boys who've been trying to up their game recently." The cop smirked. "Would probably have gotten a bounty after this job, but... Guess you're out of a payday, Mr. Brownstone."

"It wasn't a tough fight anyway. I've run into stray cats who put up worse fights."

The cops chuckled.

"Stick around for a few minutes," one of the cops requested. "We're going to need you to answer a few questions."

"Sure."

The cops near James stepped away to help corral the scared bank customers. The tiny cashier waved at James with a grateful smile.

The bounty hunter didn't care about any of that right now. He had a bigger problem. He stomped toward the corner where Alison remained crouched behind the potted ficus.

The girl stood as he approached.

"What are you doing here?" James asked.

The teen shrugged. "Watching you kick butt?"

"How much of it can you even see? It's not like guns have souls."

Alison shrugged. "I could see your and the bad guys' souls, and I could hear everything."

James groaned and rubbed the back of his neck. "Look, I stopped these guys, and that was a good thing, I guess, but you shouldn't be putting yourself in danger. Not yet. Not until you learn the toad spell or whatever."

"'Toad spell?'"

"I don't know. Something to turn a guy into a toad."

Alison laughed and lifted her pendant. "Besides, I have this if I need protection."

"That should be a last resort, not an excuse to charge in after me when I'm dealing with three armed men." James pointed toward the downed criminals. "And I got lucky that they weren't tougher and didn't have magic or grenades or something. For all you knew, these guys could have been like King Pyro on steroids."

She shook her head. "I don't think so. I'm getting better at seeing that sort of thing. If they had that kind of magic, I would have been able to see it in their auras."

James scrubbed a hand over his face. "I just don't want you putting yourself in danger."

"But aren't you wanting me to be more independent?"

The girl planted her hands on her hips, her face defiant.

Guess all dads of teens have to deal with this sort of shit eventually. Well, maybe not telling your teen to avoid potential firefights in banks, but same idea.

The bounty hunter let out a defeated sigh. "I've got to talk to the cops for a bit. Stick around, and don't go running into any more danger."

"Yes, sir, James." Alison gave him a bright smile.

Fuck. I really wish Shay were here to talk to about this shit.

4

The rest of the weekend continued without James having to punt anyone else into counters or estimate magazine sizes. No criminals were stupid enough to commit any crimes right in front of him, so he didn't feel any pressure from Alison to go all Brownstone on them.

The bounty hunter and the teen didn't do anything more dangerous than ride in a suspicious Lyft and try some street food. James had to admit seeing the Statue of Liberty up close was cool, even though he hadn't realized until they'd taken the ferry over to the island that Alison suggested it only for his benefit. Statues aren't of great interest to blind people.

James reflected on recent events in silence as he barreled down I-95. Their weekend of family fun had taken its toll, leaving the girl exhausted and napping on their way back to her school.

I think I'm almost as tired as when I was escaping all those hitmen.

He chuckled quietly. It wasn't that long ago that his weekends consisted of him kicking ass, spending time at confession, or relaxing with his dog and watching a few cooking shows. Between Alison, Mack, and Shay, the bounty hunter was starting to have something resembling a social life.

Not only that, he also held an important gift for Alison. Her Drow mother had entrusted him with her legacy—a wish—to bestow on her daughter when the time was right. That wish had drawn the Harriken's interest to both the mother and the daughter. James controlled the wish now, which bound him to the girl even without the emotional connection.

James took the time to think about what had happened in the bank. He'd ignored it for most of the weekend, but now couldn't help but wonder if he'd been wrong about what had been bothering Alison.

He'd assumed the issue was that she was scared of him having such a dangerous job. That she'd prefer if he quit and took up barbeque professionally or something. The stunt in the bank made him wonder if the opposite were true; if he was making the dark job seem cool and alluring.

Alison didn't seem like the kind of person who would want to become a bounty hunter, but his stomach tightened and his heart rate kicked up as he thought about their similarities. He'd been young once as well, and it wasn't as if he'd been told from his earliest days that he'd become a bounty hunter.

Both Alison and James were orphans with unusual abilities, and they had both been left completely alone in the world by acts of violence, even if other people had later decided to look after them.

Am I a bounty hunter because that's what I do best and it allows me to give back? Or is all this shit just revenge for Father Thomas? Or hell, for my parents. Some fuckers probably slit their throats.

James sped up after checking for any sign of the highway patrol.

I don't have magic myself, but I'm stronger than any man should be, and I can move shit with my mind if I want. Was I born this way, or did the amulet make me this way?

James grunted at the thought. He was strong and fast—that much was true. But he could have used his physical abilities in a number of jobs: cop, soldier, bodyguard. Even sports.

Instead, he'd chosen a career that pointed him straight at the worst parts of society. Even the police didn't always have to deal with pieces of shit. No one offered a bounty for helping people; they only paid for taking down criminal scum.

Revenge, huh? Probably. Is that a bad thing, Father Thomas? I normally try not to kill them...and they'd just hurt more people if I didn't take them down.

Alison...she's half-Drow, and even without the wish she'll probably grow into a powerful woman. She'll be way more powerful than me. Maybe she'll want revenge against the darkness too. Would it be a bad thing if she used her abilities to stop those who would abuse theirs?

James' hands tightened on the steering wheel and he took several deep breaths. The idea of the girl leaving school to follow in his footsteps set his stomach churning.

Shit, what the fuck am I thinking? I shouldn't even remotely want her anywhere near this job. Just because I'm fucked up doesn't mean she shouldn't grow up less fucked up. She's got me and Shay to help her, and her friends at school.

I need to protect her, not lead her toward shit.

James spared a glance at the sleeping girl. The white in her hair had grown since he last saw her, even if dark hair still dominated. The white indicated her heritage and the power within her small body.

You don't have to make the same mistakes I did, kid. You can be better than me. And I want to make sure you will be.

Alison yawned and stretched several hours later as James pulled into the circle drive at her school.

"We're here, kid," James rumbled. "I'll get your sh...stuff out of the back." He hopped out of the Toyota and hurried to the back to pull out her suitcases.

A frown spread on his face when he spotted Top Hat Ferret about twenty yards away. The world's most fashionably-dressed mustelid stood there, his little furry hands under his waistcoat. He glanced James' way with something like a smirk, but it was hard to tell, then turned and waved at a nearby girl before wandering off.

Fucker. Now you have a vest too? What's the point of the vest if you're not gonna wear anything else besides the hat?

James tried to shake his ferret concerns out of his head and lifted Alison's suitcases to the curb. "Do you need me to take you to your room?"

"No, I'm good."

Quick movement caught his attention, and the bounty hunter resisted the urge to grab his gun before Top Hat Ferret or some witch or wizard blasted him with a spell.

For all he knew, guns didn't even work on campus. The memory spells that redirected people who showed up without permission proved the kind of power floating around on the campus.

Instead of drawing his weapon, James slowly surveyed the area around him. He spotted several people hurrying away from the circle drive, some even running. A few moments passed before he realized it wasn't *people* running, but specifically boys. The various girl students walked or chatted around the circle drive with no concern at all. A few pointed and laughed at the boys.

"What's going on? Do all the boys have some special meeting or something?" James asked. "They are all running like a dragon's gonna bite their ass."

Alison laughed. "No, they don't have a meeting or anything" She smirked. "It's kind of my fault, actually."

"Your fault?" He glowered. "They hazing you? If so, they better f... I'll go have a talk with them."

The girl waved her hands in front of her face. "No, no, no, it's nothing like that. They're just scared."

"Of you?" James growled. "Then I *definitely* need to have a talk with them. Little punks."

Alison shook her head. "Nope. No one's afraid of me. I can barely even do magic yet." She shrugged. "But, you know, after that stuff in LA, you're kind of famous. I read an article. There're like fan sites for you."

"'Fan sites?'"

"Yeah, there's one called 'The Scourge of the Harriken.'"

She laughed. "There're a lot of thirsty women on that website who are interested in you."

James frowned. "I don't think you should be going to places like that."

"Okay, okay. I promise I won't again." The smirk on her face suggested Alison might ignore his order.

"Wait." James rubbed his forehead. "I don't get it. These boys are all scared because they know what happened with the Harriken? I'm doubting there are any bounties here. They get that I'm a bounty hunter, right? It's not like I just kill random people."

Alison giggled. "Again, my fault. It's 'cause I've told everyone my dad is James Brownstone, and that you're kind of overprotective. I mean, what boy wants to risk making the Scourge of the Harriken mad?"

James stared at her, stunned.

Alison gave him a quick hug. "Okay, I'm going to get back to my room and try to get some stuff set up for tomorrow. I loved spending time with you. Maybe next time Aunt Shay can come."

"Yeah, yeah," James replied absentmindedly. "I'm sure she would like that."

After another quick hug, the girl rolled her suitcases away.

James stared after her.

Dad. He'd started thinking of himself that way, but he hadn't known Alison had as well. He didn't know how to even *think* about being someone's dad, but he did know one thing.

He damned well liked the sound of it. And, for that matter, "Scourge of the Harriken."

Sergeant Jackson Mack spent his days processing bounties. He was used to confronting and dealing with some of the most awful beings Earth and Oriceran had to offer. On most days shit didn't bother him, but as he paced back and forth in front of the door of the small studio apartment his heart thundered.

The cop liked to think of James Brownstone as his friend, as much as a man could be a friend to a force of nature. He'd helped the bounty hunter out on a few occasions—including renting him the apartment after the destruction of his home—but Jackson didn't know if asking for a favor would be going too far.

Still, Brownstone had been gone all weekend, and now that he was finally back, it was as good as time as any to ask.

"Fuck it. I need to stop being a pussy. It's not like Brownstone's going to beat me down for asking. And the roast's getting cold." The cop knocked on the door and waited.

A moment later the door swung open, revealing the bounty hunter in a tank top with all his ridiculous muscles on display.

Shit. Better not let my woman see him like that.

"Hey, Brownstone." The cop nodded.

The bounty hunter nodded back. "What's up?"

"I had a favor to ask. Want you to go after a bounty."

Brownstone chuckled. "It's not a favor to ask me to do my job."

"Yeah, but this guy, Xander Stevens...he's not worth your time."

The bounty hunter's face scrunched in confusion. "I think you lost me, Mack."

"This guy Stevens—he's a level-one bounty, so worthless you won't earn enough to purchase toilet paper to clean off the shit from touching him."

"Yeah, you're not really selling this. Guys like that... Fuck, I normally don't even get out of bed for less than a level-three."

The cop nodded. "Yeah, I know. That's why I'm asking this as a favor."

Brownstone stared Jackson for a second. "Why do you care so much about a level-one bounty?"

"Because the fucker's hiding, and he has info related to a case where a cop was killed. We got people looking for him, but you got all sorts of channels we don't. Just your name makes shit happen, and we need this guy."

"Okay," Brownstone agreed. "Send the information to me. I've got your back, Mack. I'll find this little shit and bring him in."

5

Shay watched Brownstone as he sat on her couch. She hadn't figured that a simple weekend visit with Alison would have left him so confused. If she'd known the bounty hunter was going to have so much trouble, she'd have made more of an effort to rearrange her schedule.

The man had stopped by about twenty minutes earlier to discuss what had happened over the weekend, including the incident at the bank. That, in particular, left him more than a little worried about his influence on the girl.

"You're overthinking this, Brownstone," Shay told him, leaning back in her chair. "You're not corrupting some poor innocent girl. She's a teenager who's interested in exciting things, and even if she'd never met you she'd be doing stupid shit. That's what teens do, and if she doesn't end up a teenage professor-killer she'll be doing better than I did."

The bounty hunter grunted and shook his head. "I guess... She's now calling me her dad, which means I have a responsibility. I *have* to fucking protect her. Shit, I might even have to protect her from myself."

"You haven't harmed that girl. You saved her from the Harriken and her dirtbag father, you've taken care of her, and you helped hook her up with that school." Shay laughed. "What's the matter? Are you so convinced that you're a piece of shit that you have to look for any evidence to prove it?"

"It's not like I'm a good guy. I've killed a lot of people."

Shay rolled her eyes. "Excuse me if I'm not weeping that assholes like Sombra and King Pyro are dead. Look, Brownstone, if the sheepdog doesn't protect the herd from the wolf, the herd gets eaten. The sheepdog is still a wolf deep down in its DNA, but it's using that aggression to protect instead of harm." She waved a hand dismissively. "Don't be so worried."

"I don't know."

"Maybe I'm the last person to be saying something like this, but you *do* you know it's okay to let people in, right?" Shay stood and headed toward her kitchen. "And that girl can see souls. If you were a piece of shit she would have seen it, and if you even *look* like you're becoming a piece of shit she'll know. Maybe you should trust her."

The field archaeologist headed into the kitchen to pour herself some wine from an open bottle. "Want any?"

Brownstone glanced over his shoulder and shook his head. "Nah, I'm okay."

Shay finished pouring and took a large gulp before refilling her glass. She walked back into the living room, passing behind him on the couch. On impulse, she leaned over and kissed Brownstone on the top of his head.

The man glanced up at her with a faint look of confusion, but nothing approaching anger or discomfort.

Is that too much? Don't know if I care anymore. Maybe I should take my own damned advice about opening up.

"You're a good man, Brownstone," she assured him quietly. "Maybe the only one in this whole rotten town."

"Plenty of good people out there," Brownstone argued, looking down at the floor. "It's about where you look."

Shay sauntered over to her chair, took a seat, and crossed her legs. She took another sip of her wine before speaking again. "What do you mean?"

"You're like me. You've spent your life staring at scumbags, which makes it hard at times to remember that not everyone's a scumbag. A lot of people have helped me lately." He furrowed his brow. "And they didn't do it because they were afraid of me. Shit, even the gang that searched the remains of my house for my shit did it more out of respect than fear. Mack's giving me a place to live. The Professor may drink half the alcohol in the county, but he's always trying to keep artifacts from nasty pieces of shit." Brownstone shrugged. "He's probably a better man than I am."

Shay sighed and shook her head. "Just let me deal with you being a good man first. I understand the second time's easier."

Grandfather looked at the gathered Harriken leaders kneeling before the table in the dim light provided by a single floating orb. In the days since their last meeting he'd taken the time to plan and decide on the choice of action, and now they needed to be informed.

"Soon, killers will be coming to Tokyo," the man began. "Killers who will serve as our swords and spears."

Kodaka, the leader of Harriken operations in South Korea, looked up. "I don't understand, Grandfather."

"What's not to understand? It's a simple concept."

"We already paid killers to go after Brownstone and he killed or captured them. How will this be different?"

Several of the gathered men nodded their agreement. Others just waited, their faces impassive, as if they expected Grandfather to signal one of the silent guards lining the walls to kill Kodaka for his mild rebuke.

Grandfather shook his head. "No. Before we offered a bounty, made it a public spectacle, and invited vermin in on the chase. That was foolish, and it allowed Brownstone to control the situation. It was also an insult to true professionals." He ran a finger along the arm of his chair. "I've invited several of these true professionals—assassins of exquisite skill and experience. They will require a premium compared to the bounty, but investing in these people will allow us to kill Brownstone, if not take him alive."

"Are you sure that we should risk trying to take him alive?" Kodaka asked.

"We risk nothing more than these assassins. A sword might break in a battle, but if it takes the life of the enemy it doesn't matter. A simple death for Brownstone might not be enough for us to recover our honor. He must be made to suffer, and others must know he suffered so they know the price of defying the Harriken. He will be most properly chastised for his disrespect." He chuckled quietly. "It's simple. When facing a monster you must use a monster, so I will be hiring five."

Shay skimmed through various messages and forums as she considered possible tomb-raider jobs. James sat on the couch skimming through bounties on the LAPD Bounty Hunter Outreach app.

She forced down a laugh at a sudden realization.

When did I start spending so much time just hanging out with Brownstone? Isn't this cozy? Sure, we're looking for work, but it's a little...domestic. Is this just our thing now?

Shay peeked over her phone at Brownstone. He had a bored look on his face, which was cute in a Brownstone kind of way. Plus, when he shifted just right she couldn't help but appreciate his thick, corded muscles.

She licked her lips but then grimaced, hoping he hadn't noticed.

Down, girl. We're just friends and partners—nothing more. Maybe he's gay, maybe he's not. Maybe there's only enough room in his heart for barbecue.

No law against looking, though.

"Anything interesting?" Shay asked. "I mean, any guys who are just screaming to have their asses kicked?"

"Things have been light lately, at least for the level threes and above. A lot of the big bounties are staying out of town, and I don't want to waste time going after the garbage bounties."

"Gee, I wonder why so many scumbags decided LA's a

bad place to hang out?" Shay grinned. "Maybe there's such a thing as being too successful."

James grunted. "Can always take a trip, I guess." He returned his attention to the bounty app.

Shay decided to stop looking for tomb-raider jobs and skim a few dark web forums that catered to her previous career as a professional killer. While she had zero interest in taking on any assassination contracts, she liked to check them every once in a while to assure that no one had figured out she was still alive and placed a contract on her or Peyton, her research assistant whose death she had also faked.

"Oh, shit," she exclaimed after a few minutes.

James looked up from his phone. "What's wrong?"

"Big call for platinum-grade assassins to go to Tokyo." Shay sucked in a breath and shook her head. "Fuck, this isn't good."

"So what? I'm sure there are plenty of great bounty hunters in Japan. When I talked about taking a trip, I didn't mean to Japan. I meant down to Mexico or to Texas or some shit like that. Maybe Canada?" He frowned. "Why do they have so few decent bounties?"

"Probably all the maple syrup, but that shit isn't important." Shay waved a hand. "Connect the dots, Brownstone. It's not clear who the client is from these forums, but I'm pretty sure this means the Harriken are done playing. No one throws around this kind of money without a super-big score to settle."

The bounty hunter snorted. "You call placing a half-million-dollar bounty on me playing around?"

"Yeah, I do." Shay set her phone on the table in front of

her couch. "Look, take it from a former professional killer who was damned good at her job: you want to annoy someone, you do shit like that bounty. A top-level pro doesn't get involved in messes like the Great Brownstone Hunt. Too many variables, too much shit that can go wrong. One minute you might be setting up to take a guy down and the next you run into another hitman or a jumpy cop." She tapped the phone. "The kind of killers they want in Japan aren't gonna be idiots trying to run you off the road or the kind who get led on some wild goose chase into a pack of Marines. These fuckers don't let ego or simple greed trip them up."

Brownstone pocketed his phone. "Everything those fuckers have thrown at me I've been able to deal with. If they want to have an assassin convention in Tokyo, big fucking deal. Why should I be worried?" He shrugged.

"*We* need to deal with this. If you wait for these guys to get all set up it'll be a lot more than your house that gets blown up, especially if they come at you when you don't have the cops and the Marines watching your back. And that's if they just come at *you*."

The bounty hunter frowned. "What are you getting at?"

"The point is, tough as you are, even *you* weren't ready for them to blow up your house. At the pay level they're offering, we'll probably get some magic ability, or at least the ability to deal with magic." Shay narrowed her eyes. She'd not pressed him about the insane level of protection he got from the strange amulet she'd seen him use. "And we both know how ruthless the Harriken are, so..."

"What?"

Shay averted her gaze. "At this level, Alison might not

be safe even at that school if we wait too long. Magic can defeat magic. We need to hit them before they decide to attack you where you're vulnerable."

An almost feral anger took over James' face. "If they even fucking *sneeze* her way I'll rip them apart."

"Like I said, we need to take this shit seriously and deal with it. Fuck, let's just do it Brownstone-style."

James snorted. "And what's that?"

"The heavy and direct application of violence until everyone's dead." Shay snickered. "I guess that's Shay-style, too."

Brownstone nodded. "You're right. But I can handle this by myself. There's no reason for you to get involved. The more you do, the more they might start coming after you."

"If we do this right, there'll be no one left to come after us. Tokyo's their base. Cut the head off the dragon and all that shit." Shay shrugged. "I'm not letting the closest thing I've had to a true family get killed," she muttered under her breath.

"Huh? Didn't catch the last part."

"Don't worry about it. You need someone to watch your back. You think like a bounty hunter, not a killer. I'm a killer."

Brownstone stared at her. "You're not a killer anymore."

"Nah, I'm still a killer. I just don't get paid to do it." Shay ran a hand through her dark hair. "Point is, I think like a killer, and I know how to gather information on people like me. You need me on this, Brownstone, and I'm not gonna take no for an answer just because you have some martyr complex all those priests at the orphanage programmed into you. You don't get to tell me what I'm allowed to give a shit about."

The bounty hunter nodded slowly. "Fair enough." He glanced down at his phone. "I wonder if I should tell Alison about her wish, or even give it to her—just in case."

Shay raised a brow. "Do you think the time is right to tell her?"

"I have no fucking clue, but it kind of feels that way."

"Then we should go to Virginia and level with her."

Brownstone stood, frowning. "Why not just call her?"

"Who the fuck knows what kind of magical wiretap shit they have going on at the school?" Shay tapped her head. "Keep in mind it's not just a magic school, but a magic school established by the *government*."

"I see what you mean. Still, I don't want to worry her. After all that shit before, it might just be more stress."

"This is serious shit, and it all leads back to her anyway. We should give her the respect of letting her in on the truth. Not knowing can be a lot worse sometimes."

"She's just a kid. She shouldn't have to deal with stuff like this."

Shay shrugged. "Life's a bitch. She shouldn't have had to deal with her father selling out her mother, but she has a positive attitude despite that. She hasn't been protected from the kind of bullshit that goes on in our world."

Brownstone grunted. "You're right." He yanked his phone out of his pocket. "Okay, gonna call her school then."

Shay walked over and placed her hand on his arm. "Look, I know you want to protect her, but trust me...

sometimes the best way to protect someone is to be totally and brutally honest with them."

"Yeah, I know, but just because I agree doesn't mean I have to like it. Fucking Harriken! I thought they finally got the damned message."

Shay snickered. "Guess we found someone even more stubborn than you."

6

Grandfather knelt in front of the small table, the only furniture in the otherwise-empty room. He wore a pleasant smile on his face as he looked at his five guests, three men and two women, all experts in their field, which was the fine art of killing. Despite his normal disdain for treating women as equals, these two had earned their place at the table through the spilling of blood.

A beautiful kimono-clad woman finished pouring tea for the Harriken leader and his guests. He gave her a quick nod and she rose, bowing deeply before hurrying from the room and sliding the door closed.

A dark-skinned man in a white suit took a sip of his tea. "Not bad," he offered, his South African accent coloring his words. "But I didn't fly all the way to Japan for tea."

Grandfather gave the man a polite smile. "No, Mr. Moses, I'm sure you didn't," he replied in English. Though his fluent English was marked by only the faintest Japanese accent, having to use the language bothered him. It was a verbal indication of failure; proof he had to ask outsiders to help the Harriken.

He would shoulder the dishonor for now, and the creative torture he would inflict on Brownstone would make him feel better about the situation. And if Brownstone died, that would be fine, too.

Five assassins. Fives virtuosos of murder: Trevor Moses from South Africa, John Candle from America, Connor Malley from England, Sabine "the Collector" Haas of Germany, and Hisa the *Kunoichi*. The Japanese assassin was so cloaked in shadows that even Grandfather didn't know her real name. He only knew the attractive young Japanese woman sitting before him in a kimono was nothing more than a construct of magic. No one alive had ever seen her true appearance.

Whether or not she was a true *kunoichi,* a female ninja, it didn't matter. She'd killed enough people to be worthy of respect. Her strength demanded it.

Grandfather took a sip of tea before continuing. "You all come highly recommended. I have personally selected you five from the many who offered to come because only you have the skills and determination for my task."

"Killing James Brownstone?" John asked. He brushed a few dark strands of hair out of his face.

The Harriken leader chuckled. "Yes."

"Why did you cancel the old bounty on him if you still wanted him dead?"

"It was leading to unnecessary complications."

"I don't work for under a million," Sabine informed him, her icy blue eyes irritated.

"Nor should you," Grandfather agreed. "So I will make

the offer now, so you know that I'm not wasting your time. Two million if you kill Brownstone and five million if you bring him in alive. Not only that, I will pay in Euros, not American dollars."

Connor sipped his tea but didn't say anything. Hisa also remained silent but hadn't bothered to pick up her tea. Normally Grandfather would have been insulted, but he didn't have time to worry about social courtesies. If the woman could kill Brownstone it would be apology enough. If not, she would die at his hands and her rudeness would be punished anyway.

"Why so much more to take him alive?" Trevor asked.

"I wish to have some...entertainment with Mr. Brownstone before he dies. I have access to excellent doctors who can do a good job keeping him alive while I make him suffer."

"So that's it? Just hunt down this Brownstone?"

"It won't be as trivial as you think, but then again, that's why I've selected specialists. I will provide you with as much information as I have on the man. Use it however you want. I don't care how you do it. I don't care about collateral damage or innocent people dying. I only care that James Brownstone is either killed or brought to me."

The Harriken leader picked up his tea and took another sip with a relaxed look on his face.

The arrow has been loosed, Brownstone. Just pick where you want to die.

James, Shay, and Alison had just ordered. They were in the

Rolling Hills Barbecue Pit Stop, having driven a good thirty miles from the school with only the briefest of conversations.

James could see the tension on the girl's face, but he wanted to wait for the right time—and more importantly, until he knew it was safe. Peyton had confirmed the Harriken were behind the call for premium assassins, which meant his ass-kicking plan had become more urgent.

"You guys were both very mysterious on our way here," Alison began. "I can't believe you flew all the way to Virginia to take me to a barbecue place." She glanced at Shay and James, suspicion coloring her features. "Remember, I'm pretty good at telling when people are lying to me. I can see the worry in your souls."

James grunted. "We flew to Virginia to talk to you about some important stuff, but I figured it would be best if we got something to eat first."

He shrugged. He'd offered her nothing but the truth.

"Why couldn't we have talked at school? We could have eaten in the cafeteria."

"I've been wanting to check this place out. We'll have plenty of time to talk, and there are other reasons." James looked at Shay.

"Because we can't trust they don't have some magical spy-spell set up," Shay said. "Speaking of which, might as well take care of what we can. Peyton hooked me up with a little something that can help." She smiled and brought three small silver pyramid-shaped devices out of her jacket pocket.

She placed two on one edge of the table and the other at

the opposite end before pulling out her phone and tapping away. A triumphant grin grew on her face.

"What the hell are those things?"

"Listen," Shay ordered.

James shrugged and watched her for a moment. "Don't hear anything."

"Yeah, that's the point. It's disrupting sound waves. Someone might be able to read our lips, but at least they can't easily hear us. I can shut it off when he comes so the waiter doesn't get suspicious."

"And you don't think he'll wonder why we have weird sh...stuff on the table?"

Shay snorted. "He won't care."

She tapped her phone again and the chatter from the rest of the room returned. Now that James was listening for it, he was shocked by how much the devices filtered out.

Alison looked at the two of them. "So should we start talking about whatever is going on?"

James shook his head. "Food first, then talk. By the way, one of the reasons I picked this place was because they had great salads. I know you and Shay aren't all that hot on barbecue, but you ordered ribs."

"I've been learning more about Drow at the school," Alison said. "One of the things I've read is that they are big meat-eaters, so I've been wondering if some of the issues with my magic are because I don't eat enough meat. I figure maybe I need more protein or something." She sighed. "So, I know you want to wait until after we eat, but at least tell me what's this about."

"We need to talk about our future."

"All of our futures," Shay added.

James was about to say something else when he spotted the waiter and another coming with their food. The future could wait until they'd polished off their ribs.

After they finished with their main meal Shay reactivated the sound absorbers. Despite Brownstone's concerns, the waiter hadn't so much as glanced in the direction of the devices. In an age where everyone carried a gadget, a few extras didn't stand out.

"Okay, spill it already," Alison demanded, biting her lip. "What *about* my future? Do...do you want me to leave the school?"

Brownstone shook his head after a quick glance at Shay. "No, no. The school's perfect for you. Like that stuff you learned about Drow and meat. It's got nothing to do with school."

"Then what?"

"The Harriken didn't learn their lesson. Either of their lessons." Brownstone shrugged. "They didn't take their ass-kickings too well, and it's come down to them against me, and only one of us can continue to exist. Shay and I think the only way to end this crap is to take the pain to them in Japan."

Alison sighed and slumped in her seat. "I don't understand all this. These people killed my mom, and they just keep coming back."

Brownstone took a deep breath and looked at Shay. She

could see the hesitation on his face and gave him a slight nod.

"That's the other thing," he continued. "If we don't finish them off, there's a big chance they'll come after you."

Alison blinked. "Why? Do they hate Drow that much?"

"Nope. I'm gonna tell you something I maybe should have told you a long time ago."

"What?"

"The truth is, all this started with your dad, sure, but it wasn't just that he was a greedy ass. It goes deeper than that. It was about something special your mom had."

"Her magic? Some magical artifacts?"

Brownstone shook his head and took another deep breath. Shay patted him on the shoulder, hoping to give him a little bit of support. The man could beat people down without hesitation, but telling the girl the truth about her mother was proving a big challenge.

"No, a wish," he replied.

"A *wish?*" Alison's face twisted in confusion.

"Yep, a wish. An actual honest-to-goodness wish. Your mother, as a Drow princess, had a legacy: a wish. That was what the Harriken wanted. That was why they kidnapped her and planned to kidnap you—to force her to give them the wish. That's the thing…it has to be freely given. They couldn't force it out of her."

"But Mom was too strong for them."

"Yeah. They tried, but they failed."

"I guess you can't wish someone back to life," the girl mused. "Otherwise, Mom could have used it on herself."

Brownstone shrugged. "I honestly don't know, kid. Only know what she told me."

"Doesn't matter, I guess. The only thing important is that she died, taking the wish with her." Alison sighed. "Died stopping those bad guys from getting something important."

Brownstone shook his head. Shay swallowed, and her heart beat faster. Now was the moment of truth.

"Your mom *did* give the wish freely to someone, just not the Harriken."

Alison tilted her head, confused for a few seconds, then gasped. "*You* have it, James?"

"Yeah. She gave it to me to hold onto. Told me to give it to you when the time was right."

Shay cleared her throat. "Gave it to him by kissing him, by the way."

Alison shot a glance at the tomb raider before returning her attention to James. "And you think the time is right?"

"Hell if I know, but I'm about to fly halfway around the world to take on some bad guys on their turf and in their home country. I need to give it to you before I leave because if the worst happens your inheritance shouldn't die with me."

"Back up a bit," the girl requested. "My mom *kissed* you?"

Brownstone groaned. "Yeah, but it was about transferring the wish. Mostly. I think."

"Sure. Their lips were locked like she was the *Titanic* and he was the iceberg," Shay grumbled.

Alison laughed and stared at the field archaeologist for a moment. Shay shifted under her attention.

Shit, she can see right through me. I wonder if jealousy really is green.

Shay waited for Alison to mention her feelings, but instead the girl looked back at Brownstone.

"Keep the wish," the teen told him with a smile. "I don't need it."

A look of discomfort covered Brownstone's face. "I, uh, kid... Maybe you're not understanding."

"No, James. I understand fine. My only wish is that you come back, and if you need the wish to help with that, I want you to use it."

Brownstone gave Shay a pleading look.

The tomb raider rolled her eyes. "If you don't like the idea, just come back without needing it, dumbass."

7

By the time they dropped Alison off, James felt even less comfortable than before they'd talked to the girl. She seemed happy about the whole thing, but he still had trouble wrapping his mind around the idea of her being more concerned about him than receiving her mother's legacy.

I'm not worth someone's wish. I'm just a bounty hunter.

James pulled into the circle drive, confusion still filling his mind. They all stepped out of the rental car, another Toyota. A sharp memory cut through the confusion, and he figured he should face the implications before he left.

"Alison," he began. "There was something else I wanted to talk to you about."

Shay eyed him with a frown, and he just shrugged. She probably assumed he was going to talk about something that required her sound absorbers.

"What?" Alison asked.

"Last time I was here, you said you were telling people I was your dad."

The teen nodded slowly, anxiousness creeping onto her face. "That's not a problem, is it? I know you're not...like *really* my dad, but I think of you like that and I like the idea. You've done a lot more for me than Walt ever did." Venom filled her voice when she mentioned her biological father.

James took a deep breath and slowly let it out. Tightness attacked his shoulders and neck.

Shit. I don't think I was this nervous when I fought that army of zombies.

"Look, kid," the bounty hunter continued. "You don't have to call me dad, but I would be honored if you did. If...*when* I get back, we can do the paperwork if you want. I want to adopt you."

Alison rushed over and threw her arms around him as tears leaked out of her eyes.

James looked at Shay in panic and confusion and the tomb raider rolled her eyes for about the twentieth time that day.

"She's happy, you idiot," she mouthed.

The comment smothered the panic and confusion, which left only satisfaction.

James patted Alison on the head, not giving a shit or feeling any embarrassment at the glances or stares of anyone around them.

Shay stepped behind him and rubbed his back.

Protection. That was all he could think about; protecting Alison and Shay.

I'm not that little boy now, Father Thomas. I don't need you to protect me anymore. I can protect the people I care about.

For the first time in a long time James could see a future, something that wasn't just pain and violence broken by the occasional barbecue feast.

A family. He almost wanted to laugh at the idea. He'd given up on the idea long ago, thinking no one could love an ugly and cursed freak like him, but Shay and Alison had both accepted him with all his faults and sins.

Only one obstacle remained: the Harriken. The bastards wanted to take that happy future from them.

Fuck you. You want me? You can have me right after I finish you off once and for all.

"You okay, Brownstone?" Shay asked as they hit the highway to return to the airport.

Even the tomb raider's cold heart had been moved by the earlier scene. She couldn't say she understood everything about the bounty hunter, but she could relate to the pain and loneliness he lived with most of his life.

During her years as a killer, Shay had formed few real friendships. One of her friends had come to kill her on the fateful night Shay decided to walk away from the job. Lovers and children seemed more distant than Mars. For a woman who swam in blood, it seemed absurd to worry about something as positive as love and happiness.

Now, though, something better seemed just within reach. A lasting light instead of a clinging gloom.

I'm not a good woman, and I've done a lot of bad things. I know I don't deserve to be happy. Doesn't mean I don't want to go for it.

Brownstone grunted. "Just need to finish up this Harriken bullshit so I don't need to have more conversations like that with Alison."

"You did the right thing, leveling with her."

"I don't know what the right thing is anymore, other than making sure she doesn't have to worry about people she cares about dying. Plus, these Harriken fuckers are really starting to get annoying."

"So they weren't annoying when they blew up your house?"

"That was inconvenient. This is downright annoying."

Shay's phone beeped and she glanced down at it. It was a text from her research and hacking assistant, Peyton—yet another person she could call a true friend in her new life.

Got the info you asked for. Check your private site, normal password and shit.

"Huh. That was fast," Shay remarked.

"What?" Brownstone asked.

"I had Peyton hit the net hard to grab what he could about who ended up partying with the Harriken after their hiring spree. Give me a sec to check out the information. I want to see what we're dealing with."

Shay swiped and tapped at her phone, furrowing her brow as she scanned the information sent by Peyton. Her Man-Puppy could be annoying at times, but he was great at finding information and presenting it efficiently.

Brownstone glanced Shay's way after a few minutes. "So what's the score?"

"Five killers, it looks like. All top-grade. Peyton's got confirmation that four are definitely in Japan, but he's not sure if they are still waiting for the fifth person to show up or if she's just really good at hiding her trail."

"Five?" Brownstone snorted. "That's it? I dealt with more hitmen last time. I thought the Harriken would up their game."

"Keep that confidence, Brownstone. It'll either get you killed or help you roll right through these guys. I wouldn't be so blasé, though."

"Why?"

"I keep telling you these aren't just hitmen. These are premium top-grade assassins. True killers; some of the best in the business. The only reason most of them don't have bounties is that they're so good the authorities can't actually prove they've been involved in any of their killings." Shay tapped on her phone as she scanned the information Peyton sent her. "Trevor Moses, John Candle, Connor Malley, Sabine Haas, and Hisa the *Kunoichi*."

"*Kunoichi?*"

"Female ninja."

Brownstone groaned. "The ones with special nicknames are always extra-fucking-obnoxious. She's probably gonna rant at me about how she's the ultimate ninja or some shit."

"Tough types with nicknames are obnoxious?"

"Yeah. Like King Pyro or Sombra."

"Or the Granite Gargoyle or Granite Ghost?"

Brownstone let out a quiet chuckle. "Okay, I'll give you that."

Shay chuckled. "I never had a nickname when I was a killer, but I was still obnoxious."

"Was? Don't you mean you still are?" Brownstone

glanced her way before returning his attention to the road. "Which one is missing? You said *her*. Sabine or Hisa?"

"Hisa."

Brownstone frowned. "But she's Japanese. Shouldn't we expect her to be there?"

"Brownstone, when you're a high-end killer you go where the work is. A good chunk of my jobs were outside the United States when I was on the job. Why do you think I learned so many languages?"

"To shop easier in France?"

"It does help, but seriously, Brownstone, we can't be certain if she's there."

Brownstone nodded. "Good point. So, we got any info on what these assholes are capable of other than having nicknames?"

"Moses likes poisons, but he's not a magical guy. Candle…" Shay made a face.

"What?"

"I've heard of him before. This guy's the worst of both worlds."

"What the fuck does that mean?"

Shay sighed. "His abilities… Well, people aren't a hundred percent sure if it's tech or magic or both, but most think it's both. He uses guns. That's normal enough, but he can do shit with his guns that shouldn't be possible even for the best shot in the world."

"Like what? Shooting a dime out of the air at a hundred yards?"

"Nope, more like shooting around a corner at ninety degrees. Hit people without looking at them. That sort of shit. He uses a couple of guns that have these weird glowing runes on them, so it's a good bet they have been enchanted."

"Fucking magic. Anything about his bullets penetrating deeper or causing more damage? Magical armor-piercing or that kind of shit?"

Shay looked back down at her phone. "Not that I've heard of, and Peyton's notes don't say anything about it."

"He won't be a problem, then."

"A guy who can shoot around corners won't be a problem?" Shay snorted. "You can see through walls now, Brownstone?"

"As long as I'm properly prepared I can take a bullet or two, and we're hunting them just as much as they're hunting me. I think I'll be ready when I take him on."

The tomb raider stared at the man for a moment. Taking a bullet or two was an understatement. She'd seen him take a full load of buckshot to the chest at point-blank range and only look annoyed. Still, other times he seemed just as vulnerable as everyone else. She had her theories on why, but she planned to wait until Brownstone broached the issue.

"What else we got?" the bounty hunter asked as he changed lanes to pass a slow-moving truck.

"Connor Malley's some sort of electricity guy."

Brownstone snorted. "If I can deal with a flame guy I can deal with an electricity guy. Is the guy immune to bullets?"

"Nope."

"Then he'll go down easily enough, just like the last few magical assholes who didn't use shields."

Shay nodded. Brownstone had proven he could go

against enhanced and magical individuals countless times, but her heart wouldn't settle down from the earlier worry.

"You good against poison, Brownstone?" she asked.

"Maybe."

"'*Maybe*?' What kind of fucking answer is that? Yes or no?"

"I don't sit around drinking Drano all day, so how the fuck do I know? I'm good with alcohol. That's a poison."

Shay rubbed the back of her neck. "So of those three, the main threat is probably Trevor Moses. Even if you can take some damage or whatever, he might be able to take you out with a little prick."

"I'll bet he *has* a little prick."

"I'm serious, Brownstone."

The bounty hunter grunted. "I'll just blow his brains out before he can poison me. You know how I like to KISS. I've also got a new combat philosophy: ABA."

"'ABA?'"

"Always be attacking. That's KISS combat in a nutshell."

Shay snorted. "Whatever. The women are just as dangerous as the men, so don't get too cocky."

Brownstone smirked. "Yeah, I know how dangerous a stubborn woman killer can be."

"Keep it up and I'll do their work for them long before we get to Tokyo."

They both chuckled.

"Anyway, Hisa's a real problem because she's got some sort of illusion magic that lets her change her appearance. No one knows what she really looks like. It's gonna be hard to guard against someone who can look like anyone. Almost, anyway."

Brownstone grunted. "Almost?"

"Only real restriction Peyton could dig up is that her magic only lets her take on female appearances."

"Oh, so she could only be *half* the world, not the entire world. That really fucking narrows it down."

Shay grinned. "Right?"

"What about that Sabine chick?"

"You're gonna love this. She's got a nickname."

Brownstone shook his head and glanced into the rearview mirror. "Of course she does."

"'Sabine the Collector.'"

"What's she collect? Heads? Kills?"

Shay's smile disappeared. "Not from what Peyton could tell. She collects souls."

Brownstone's face darkened. Even if Shay wasn't as religious as the bounty hunter, the idea that someone might snatch someone else's most fundamental essence left her stomach twisting.

"So what does this bitch do with the souls?" Brownstone growled.

"Puts them in this magic necklace she has," Shay replied.

An uncomfortable look spread over the bounty hunter's face. "And what then?"

"It's supposed to give her a lot of ass-kicking power." She stared into the mirror in the sun visor. "In terms of direct danger, Trevor Moses and Sabine are probably the big threats. Hisa might be if she can catch you off-guard, but we don't know how tough she is in a fight."

"Need some sort of plan," Brownstone rumbled. "Some way to take the fight to them."

"Peyton's doing his best to track them, but I think the next major step is gonna be us going to the Land of the Rising Sun to deliver some pain."

"If I kill these fuckers, do you think more killers will take contracts on me?" Brownstone glanced her way, anger on his face.

"I think if we wipe out the Harriken and you kill five of the top people in the field, the underworld will get the point. Look, Brownstone...killers might like the job, but they still are in it to make money. It's hard to make money when you're dead."

"You ever turn down a job because it was too risky?"

"Yeah, a few times. I don't believe in ABA. I believe—well, *believed*, anyway—in ABK. Always be killing. That requires you to make sure the mark dies and not you."

A Mustang tore by them in the right lane, easily going twenty over the speed limit.

"Fucker," Shay muttered.

"Still less annoying than most days in LA."

"True enough."

Shay couldn't help but notice that ever since she'd mentioned Sabine the Collector and her necklace Brownstone had looked uncomfortable.

"Something else bothering you?" the tomb raider asked.

Brownstone passed another car before answering. "Yeah. Something is."

8

I *s it a coincidence? Some crazed assassin uses a necklace that makes her more powerful and collects souls? Fuck.*

James tried to calm his heart, but every new thought only sent it racing faster. He'd always assumed his amulet was cursed, but he also assumed the cost of its use might be his soul, at the worst.

The idea that he might be drawing on the power of *other* people's souls sent bile into his throat. There was no amount of confession that would make that okay.

"This Sabine...does she have to constantly collect souls?" he asked.

"What do you mean?"

"Does her necklace's power fade after a while or some shit like that?"

"From what Peyton's research says, yeah, she has to constantly do it. The power fades pretty quickly. Might even be why she became a killer." Shay shrugged. "Can't say for sure."

James took a deep breath. He often didn't use his amulet for long stretches at a time, and it'd had become more powerful over time.

Sounds like it's not the same thing, but it's about time I figured out what the hell it even is. If I'm gonna have any sort of future, I need to know about my past first. I've got to stop running from it.

"I need your help," James mumbled.

"I thought you already understood that I'm helping you. I've got your back, Brownstone. I'm coming with you, whatever you decide. We'll paint Tokyo red with the killers' blood, then maybe go get some sushi and sing karaoke." Shay grinned.

"It's not about that. It's something else. Research shit. You're better at that. I'm only good at tracking down bounties, not all that history stuff."

Shay frowned. "What are you talking about? What does any of that have to do with assassins?"

"Nothing. Well, not directly. It's more about the tools I might use to fight the killers."

"What do you mean?"

James took several deep breaths before he could work up the will to force the words out of his mouth. "I know you've seen it. The amulet necklace. The artifact."

The tomb raider's face twitched. "Yeah, I've seen it. Just answer me one question before we continue this conversation. Is that why you're bulletproof sometimes? Or, fuck— why you could take on someone like King Pyro and not end up a charred corpse?"

"Yeah. I just...don't know how it works, but it makes me tougher and strengthens some of my other abilities."

"Like what?"

"Telekinesis."

"What? You can move shit with your mind?" Shay shook her head. "You keep surprising the fuck out of me."

Do you still trust me, Shay, or am I some freak now to you?

James shrugged. "I don't use it much, and it's only worth anything when I have the amulet on. And now I need to know the amulet's true deal."

Shay snorted. "What the fuck do you mean by that? You're using some artifact and you don't even know how it works? Magic's just like everything else in life, Brownstone. There's always some sort of hidden cost. It could be shortening your life every time you use it."

"Probably, but it's not like I plan to live that long."

A faintly concerned look appeared on Shay's face before anger replaced it. "What about Alison? You're talking about adopting her but you don't give a shit if you're feeding your life into some Oriceran amulet?"

"I *do* care." James sighed. "That's the point. Things are different now. Shit, I was satisfied not knowing before, but... Well, I need to know now." A sign revealed that the airport was coming up soon. "I need to understand this amulet. I don't like to use the thing for a lot of reasons, but you've seen firsthand what I can do. If I knew more about it, maybe I could control it better."

He stopped before admitting the thing whispered to him in a language he didn't understand. Right now he needed Shay's trust and belief, not her paranoia.

"Where exactly do I come in?" the tomb raider asked with a curious glint in her eyes.

"You have to understand, I don't remember a lot from

when I was a kid. I don't even remember my parents. The man I thought of as my father was a priest, Father Thomas. He was killed protecting me." James shook his head. "I think that's one of the reasons I do what I do now. After he died I was given a box of my stuff, and that amulet was in it. I didn't find out for a few years what it was capable of. I figure maybe you could research it. I'm assuming it's Oriceran, but I need to know more about it. Like if it's even safe to use long-term."

"Yeah, that's kind of messed up. Anything else you can tell me about your past?"

James furrowed his brow. He didn't want to admit the next part, but if he wanted to find out the truth Shay needed more clues.

I've got to trust her more. Fuck, she's seen me at my violent worst already and hasn't turned away.

"The only thing I remember from before people found me and took me to the orphanage is that one minute I was walking in the jungle and the next I was in some dirt field. For years I thought maybe that was just a dream, but now I'm not so sure."

Shay looked down for a moment, deep in thought. "Sounds like magic. Maybe you gated or teleported somehow. Or someone gated or teleported you."

"I don't know. The people who found me said I wasn't saying words. I was just making weird clicks and pops, but I was old enough that I should have been speaking some sort of language. At least a few words." James glanced Shay's way. "Do you think you could help me research the amulet? I figure you track down magical artifacts for a living, so you know better than me how to find out the truth."

The woman took a deep breath and nodded. "Okay. When we get back I can do some research, but what about Tokyo and the Harriken?"

James shook his head. "We're not going right away. I have a couple of errands to take care of in LA before I go on any overseas adventures. We should give Peyton a little more time to nail down Hisa's location anyway."

"Okay, then, I've got a good place to start with research. I've got a lot of special books in one of my warehouses. It's not lame like the glorified storage unit you call a warehouse. It's an actual warehouse, and since we're doing the whole trust shit, I'll tell you. It's basically a library, with a lot of history and magic stuff. I call it Warehouse Four."

"So you have different warehouses?"

"Yeah…five of them."

James turned at a sign for County Road 649. "Maybe I could go with you and help you look through things. I know I'm not a research specialist, but it could help speed things up."

Shay burst out laughing. "No fucking way are you getting anywhere near my library."

"What the hell?"

The woman calmed herself and sighed. "Look, Brownstone, the shit in there is rare and expensive. I'm sorry, but you are a bull in a china shop no matter where you go, and that's when people *aren't* trying to kill you. I trust you with my life, but I don't trust that you won't fuck up my books. I can't take the chance that some exploding drone follows you and sets that place on fire." She shrugged. "A guy rolled up in a van and blew up your house, remember?"

"Yeah." James snorted. "Fair enough."

"When we get back I'll need to examine the amulet; get some pictures with my AR goggles and a couple other things. Then I can start looking through my books and online."

"Also fair enough. I can't let you take it with you. I... It's not that I don't trust you."

Shay waved a hand. "Don't worry about it. Just need pictures. We'll figure this out."

"I'm sure we will."

I just wonder if the answers will make things better or worse.

The next afternoon, Shay stood in Brownstone's glorified storage unit looking down at the amulet. It didn't look all that unusual: a circular gold and silver amulet on a silver chain. Azure, crimson, and jade crystals were inset, and it was cool to the touch.

The tomb raider had run across several more impressive artifacts in her short time in her new career. Nothing stood out about the style of workmanship to suggest a source, either Earthly or Oriceran.

Shay flipped down her goggles and took a picture with a press of a button. She switched to infrared and took more, followed by UV mode.

"What the fuck?"

"What is it?" Brownstone asked.

Shay lifted the amulet in the palm of her hand. "It's different with my UV filters."

Brownstone shook his head. "How?"

Shay ran her fingers along the edges of the amulet. "With normal vision you can't see anything besides these crystals, but when I added my UV filter I could suddenly see a bunch of little glyphs."

"Huh. I never even thought to try something like that. What do they mean?"

"I don't know offhand, but there's something familiar about them." Shay took a few more pictures from different angles. "I think we've at least got a good lead to start tracking this thing down. Let me take some more pictures, then I'll hit Warehouse Four and start the real research."

Shay smiled to herself. Brownstone appealing directly for her help proved he respected her not just as a killer, but as a tomb raider. She could build on that respect, but first she'd have to help him solve the mystery of the amulet.

Don't worry, Brownstone. I'll find out all the crazy bullshit behind your amulet.

Tyler stood behind the bar polishing glasses and smiling. Only a small number of customers were in the building that evening, but he didn't give a fuck. After his recent success with the Brownstone betting nights, he had more money than he knew what to do with. While he always liked to project a confident air, he'd been struggling for a while. With the threat of financial doom no longer hanging over him, a swagger had reentered his step.

The door swung open and the bartender turned to nod at the new arrival, but then his face twitched and indecision froze him.

Oh, fuck. Of course you'd come here to ruin my good mood, you sonofabitch.

James Brownstone pushed into the room and headed straight toward the bar, looking around the room in confusion as if it were the first time he'd been in the place.

"Lose your brain again, Brownstone?" Tyler asked, setting down the glass he'd been polishing. "Or just your sanity?"

"Maybe my memory." The bounty gestured around the room. "Last time I was in here this place looked like the ass-end of a garbage dump. Now there's a new paint job, newly-refinished bar, and new tables and chairs. New TV that's twice as big. You're not that good an information broker, Tyler. What gives?"

The bartender smirked. "You can think what you want, muscle-head, but I'm smart enough to seize opportunities when they present themselves and some of those opportunities have proven very profitable."

"And what the hell does that mean? You sell some really nice tip recently?"

Tyler leaned forward and rested his elbows on the bar. "It's not like I wasn't following your little Tour de Violence with the hitmen, asshole. That was an opportunity to make some money, so I seized it."

Brownstone glared at him. "What? You got rich selling my location to hitmen? Is that why they were always on me?"

Tyler scoffed. "No, that information was pretty much free on the net. Everyone wanted your ass dead, so they were all sharing. Value comes from scarcity, not that I'd expect you to understand a concept like that."

"But you made money off me?"

"Yeah, but I found a better way to make money."

"How?"

Tyler shrugged. "I set up a little gambling pool. Oh, it was nice. Bets on how long you would survive, how many guys you'd take out—all sorts of shit. A slice of that helped me earn a lot, but that was just the beginning."

Brownstone chuckled. "Aww, poor baby. Bet you never planned on me surviving. Must have really fucked up your profit plans."

"That's where you're wrong, asshole." Tyler laughed and shook his head. "Nah, I hedged on you living, Brownstone. Surviving like the cockroach you are. Took out a big bet myself that your ass would survive when almost no one believed it." He slapped the bar. "This is the bar that betting for and against Brownstone built. You might not have made me rich, but you've made me a lot more comfortable. Now when you go home tonight and sleep, I want you to think about how while you were out there dodging killers I was making money off your suffering."

"Couldn't have happened to a bigger asshole. Hope your bar burns down tonight."

"Whatever. Did you just come here to harass me? I'm a respectable businessman who helps the local economy by hiring contractors. You can't just come in here and harass me."

"No, Mr. Respectable Businessman. I came to ask for some information on a bounty." Brownstone nodded toward the room. "And since I made you so much money, maybe you should give me this one for free. Consider it my slice of the pool, since it was *my* life you were betting on."

"You might be a good bounty hunter, but you're a shitty businessman. You don't get rich giving away shit. Tell me what you want, and maybe I'll tell you a price or maybe I'll tell you to take a fucking hike. It's all about opportunities as far as I'm concerned."

"I need anything you can give me on Xander Stevens."

Tyler's face scrunched up in confusion. "Seriously? Are you fucking messing with me?"

"Nope. Xander Stevens."

The bartender laughed. "I heard they fined the fuck out of you, but I thought all those Harriken bounties paid it off. If you're going after level-one losers like Stevens you must be harder up than I thought. Oh, this is great."

"My bank account's just fine." Brownstone snorted. "Give me the fucking information or I'll show you how hard my fist is."

"Nah, nah. It's fine. Don't get all bitchy, now. Protecting some loser like Stevens doesn't have a lot of profit in it." Tyler pulled out a notepad and pen from a drawer and scribbled a number after consulting his phone. He slid it in front of Brownstone. "That should at least get you started." He winked. "Good luck, Brownstone. By the way, word on the street is the Harriken aren't done with you."

"Yeah, I know. Maybe you should start another betting pool."

Tyler grinned. "Nah. I don't want to press my luck. But, hey, try to not die early, just in case, you know, I change my mind."

James snatched the paper and turned to leave. "At least it doesn't smell like piss anymore."

9

James stepped out of the Black Sun and headed toward his F-350. He still found himself surprised by the impressive repair job. Everything from the handling to the paint job was as good as before, if not better. No one would ever suspect the truck had been parked right next to an exploding house and ended up with debris in the engine and pieces of wood in the windshield.

The bounty hunter checked underneath the truck just in case Tyler had someone trying something clever, and once satisfied he wasn't about to be blown up, the bounty hunter stepped inside the truck.

He was just about to put the key in the ignition when his phone rang, so he tossed the ring on the dashboard and answered it.

"Hey, Shay," James answered.

"First of all, just wanted to let you know that I got a call from Peyton. He says at least some of our new friends are on the move, or at least getting ready to be on the move."

"Where?"

"Out of Japan."

"So they're coming to party here?"

"That's what I'd assume. Can't be a hundred percent sure, though."

James grunted. "Good. It'll be easier if we deal with them on our turf. Then we'll go over there and handle the source of this shit. Do we know when they'll get here?"

"Nope. Too good at covering their tracks. Just know that some of them might be on their way. Could be one, could be all of them."

"Guess we should clear our social calendars then."

Shay chuckled. "Yeah. That's not all I called about, though. I have a few questions."

"About?"

"Your past. It'll help me with my research on your little toy. You busy?"

James shrugged reflexively even though Shay couldn't see him. "I was in the middle of something, but it's nothing that can't wait a few seconds. Ask away."

He could hear the rustle of paper over the line.

"First question: can you tell me anything more about your speech as a kid when they found you?" Shay asked. "That might help narrow things down a bit."

"I told you, I just made weird pops and clicks. I didn't speak any language. I just assumed I was making strange noises because I was scared."

"I think you might be wrong."

"Huh? What do you mean?"

"There are languages on Earth that have pops and clicks —things like Xhosa. It might not have been that you're

86

weren't speaking a language, only that you weren't speaking a language anyone understood—especially if you were teleported from somewhere far from the United States."

James had honestly never thought of the possibility. So many holes remained in his memory from when he was young. He'd never worried that much about those early dark memories, given that plenty of people couldn't remember much from when they were very young. It only was an issue because of his mysterious past and the amulet.

The bounty hunter let out a chuckle. His memory had grown better and stronger as he'd gotten older, to the point he now had an effectively photographic memory in most situations.

Was that going to happen anyway, or is my stronger memory because I've been using the amulet?

"Well, the guys at the Church weren't experts on foreign languages other than Latin," James replied. "They just said I couldn't speak English and they taught it to me. They were worried that maybe I was slow or something, but I didn't have any problems learning to speak, and picked up everything else pretty quickly too."

Shay mumbled something to herself before speaking clearly over the line. "And you said you remembered being in a jungle? Do you remember anything about it? The types of plants, the animals...anything? Even the colors? Anything you can recall might help us narrow it down to somewhere on Earth or let us know it was Oriceran. Any tiny detail."

James let out a little growl of frustration. "Been trying to think about it for years, but all I can remember is being

about the whispers.

Still, everyone had a few secrets, and the woman, much like Alison, was one of the few people he didn't want to risk pushing away. Caring this much was unfamiliar to him, and as painful as it was pleasant.

Please find the truth, Shay.

The amulet weighing on her mind, Shay drove her Fiat Spider to Warehouse Four, making sure to take a circuitous route from her home. No matter how comfortable she became with Brownstone, Peyton, and Alison, that didn't change the fact that powerful people might come after her if they realized where and who she was.

The tomb raider was worried about the Harriken, but she assumed that soon enough she and Brownstone would end that threat.

Shay parked her car underneath an overhang and walked to the recessed back door. After a quick survey of the sky to make sure there were no suspicious drones nearby, she disabled the motion sensors with her phone and unlocked the door.

Her next obstacles included a keypad and a retinal scanner, so she entered the required code and scanned her eye. The internal bolts locking the interior door retracted and she slipped into the dimly-lit main room.

The lights flicked on. Row after row of bookcases lined the walls floor to ceiling, along with several rolling ladders.

Shay inhaled deeply through her nose, enjoying the

cool air and the scent of old books, history, knowledge, and truth.

Brownstone might barbecue to relax, but Shay loved disappearing into her books.

I know I've seen those glyphs somewhere. Time to get cracking.

A couple of hours later Shay sat at a table with piles of books, some closed and stacked, others open. Printouts of the UV-enhanced images from her goggles sat on either side of an open book in front of her.

Her search hadn't brought her any closer to identifying the glyphs on the amulet.

Where have I seen these images? Not Mycenean. Not Old-Kingdom hieroglyphics. Not ancient Chinese. Not ancient Sumerian. They also don't look like a lot of the more common Oriceran scripts used during ancient contact. Elven, Gnomic, Dwarven, Atlantean...all look nothing like those glyphs.

Shay looked down at her book, a tome written in the 1920s, which chronicled a now-forgotten and lost archaeological expedition to some Egyptian pyramids headed up by one Sir Michael Garfield. The field archaeologist settled down to flip through the pages, sighing.

Was it something I've seen recently? Something I was looking up for a job? Damn it, I know I've seen them.

Thinking about her old jobs didn't narrow it down. She'd been all over the world in recent months, from Peru to Austria, and she'd also read more than a few books about areas that didn't have to do with any of her jobs.

I've been doing nothing but throwing more hay on top of the needle. Perfect.

The frustration built with each passing minute. If she'd had *no* clue about the glyphs, she would have been less bothered than with the current prickling sensation in the back of her mind of having recently seen the symbols.

"Of course Brownstone has to make this fucking complicated," she mumbled. "Why couldn't he just have an artifact with some old Elvish script on it or something? Binding shit in the darkness and all that."

Shay turned the page, ready for more disappointment, but her hand froze. She stared at the image on the page, her pulse thundering and her breathing shallow.

The picture capturing her attention wasn't the best image, given that it was a reprint of a photograph of rubbings found in the notes from the Garfield expedition. Even with all those filter layers, the fuzzy image contained several symbols that looked like stylized versions of the glyphs on Brownstone's amulet.

No fucking way.

Shay's gaze flicked back and forth between the picture in the book and the photos next to it. Each look only cemented in her mind that she was looking at the same basic symbols.

"Found you."

A quick review of the page's text discussed the mysterious lost Garfield Hieroglyphs and how scholars had decided Garfield had either recorded them incorrectly or faked them, since no other Egyptian expedition had found similar hieroglyphs.

The tomb raider gasped. She finally remembered where

she'd seen the amulet glyphs before: on pyramids, just not *Egyptian* pyramids.

What was the name of that book? I have to find it.

Shay shot up from her chair and sprinted to a nearby bookshelf. Her fingers flew along the spines until she located a book she'd read a few weeks ago, *Ancient Pyramids of Latin America*. Because of her recent jobs in South America, she'd been trying to improve her general knowledge of the area.

The tomb raider hurried back to the table and opened the book, flipping through it with such force she risked ripping the pages—normally unthinkable for a book that was over a hundred years old. Her hand shook and her pulse pounded in her ears as each page surrendered to a new one.

Shay finally stopped flipping and stared at a large print of a Toltec step pyramid. Even though the Toltec pyramid and the Egyptian pyramids mentioned in the Garfield Expedition were separated by both thousands of miles and years, they shared similar glyphs.

Too many specific details for this to be a coincidence. These had to come from a common cultural influence, but what?

The Toltec pyramid symbols, according to local informants, had been taught to the local people by beings they referred to as "the Sky Gods."

Shay shook her head, trying to think the implications through. Before the truth about Oriceran came out, many writers and scholars had attempted to tie ancient sites and artifacts to non-Oriceran aliens possessing advanced technology rather than magic.

Now, though, everyone just assumed that all those

stories weren't about Little Green Men from Alpha Centauri, but Little Not-so-Green Elves from Oriceran or similar beings. The old-school Ancient Alien Hypothesis was dismissed as something only rambling crazies believed, despite the fact that no one had a problem casually attributing many ancient mysteries to magic.

Shay snickered.

What if we just made the wrong assumptions...again? We thought we were right about history, but we didn't know what the hell we were talking about. We always want to believe the easy, neat story, and that would be that there's just Earth and Oriceran. Adding other planets with intelligent life into the mix makes things less elegant, but the truth isn't always elegant.

The tomb raider started pacing, trying to work through everything in her mind. *She* might be the one making assumptions and jumping to conclusions rather than the scholars. It wasn't impossible that some ancient Oriceran culture now long gone had left the symbols and disappeared from the history of both worlds, but there was no evidence linking the glyphs to Oriceran other than assumption.

If it's not Oriceran and it involves sky gods, that suggests another planet.

Shay stared at photos of the amulet. "Just what the hell *is* this thing?"

10

"You better not be shitting me," James growled into his phone. "I'm getting really fucking impatient. It's been a long night."

"I'm serious, man. That's Xander's number. I promise. I swear. Please just don't come after me. I ain't done shit but some dust, man."

"I'm gonna hang up now. I hope for your sake you're telling the truth, or you better start running." He ended the call.

The bounty hunter leaned back in the seat of his truck and let out a loud groan. Tyler must have been fucking with him by giving him a number he knew would lead to Xander Stevens, but not without a lot of legwork.

What had followed was a series of escalating calls and threats. Stevens probably knew James was coming for him now, but that could be a good thing. When spooked bounties ran they made a lot of noise that made them easy to track.

Tyler, you fucker, you're probably sitting there laughing at me. Doesn't matter, as long as I call this next number and it's him.

James dialed the number and the phone rang a few times.

"Hello?" a man answered.

"Xander Stevens?"

"Who is this? How did you get this number?"

I win, Tyler. I fucking win.

James chuckled. "It wasn't easy. I had to call a lot of people and ask them not so politely to get to you. Hey, you might have heard of me! I'm James Brownstone. I hear they're calling me 'the Scourge of the Harriken' now."

"Oh, fuck. Seriously? This is Brownstone?"

"Yes, seriously."

"W-why are you after me? I've read about you. You don't bother with gutter trash like me. I'm only a level-one bounty, dude." Desperation tinged the man's voice.

"Yeah, so I've heard."

"I'm not worth your time. I'm sure there's some other dude you could take out and make a lot more money."

James resisted the urge to laugh. "Yeah, I know I could, but here's how we're gonna play this. We can do this the easy way, or the fucking annoying way. And trust me, the fucking annoying way would hurt you way more than me."

Stevens swallowed audibly. "And what's the easy way?"

"You're gonna march down to the nearest police station and turn yourself in. If you do that, you don't have to deal with me smashing down your door. Sounds good, right? Everyone's a winner."

"Okay, okay. I'll do it. Just need two hours."

"Two hours?" James growled. "Why the fuck do you need two hours, asshole? Why not thirty minutes?"

"My dad," Stevens stammered. "I need to visit my dad. He's in the hospital at Cedars-Sinai. He just got out of surgery. I just want to tell him goodbye."

"Name?"

"Xander Stevens, dude."

"No, your dad's name, idiot."

"Paul Stevens."

The bounty hunter grunted. "Let's just say I value family, even when it involves assholes. Don't try and run, Stevens. You won't like it if I get angry. I'll know if you try to run, then I'll show you what it means to be the Scourge of the Harriken."

"Oh fuck, no. I get it. Can I go now, sir?"

"Sure."

Stevens hung up, and James burst out laughing.

Sir?

James gave himself a couple minutes to calm down and called the hospital.

"Cedars-Sinai Medical Center," answered a chipper receptionist.

"Yeah, just trying to send some flowers to my uncle. His name is Paul Stevens. Just wanted to know his room number."

"One moment, sir." A few seconds later the woman came back on the line. "Sir, I can confirm that Mr. Stevens is here, but HIPAA regulations prevent me from giving out his room number over the phone. If you just address the flowers to him, once they arrive we will make sure they get to him."

"That's fine. Thanks for the help."

"Anything else?"

"No, that's it. Thanks."

James hung up and cracked his neck back and forth. "Guess it's time to visit the hospital."

James lingered in the hospital parking lot a few rows down from the main entrance, waiting for Stevens to leave. The man had seemed scared enough that he shouldn't be a problem, but scared rabbits could pull off impressive escapes.

The bounty hunter glanced at the clock in his dash—only a couple of minutes until the two-hour limit was up.

James grunted, wondering what he'd do if the bounty didn't come out. It wasn't like he could storm a hospital filled with sick and injured people.

The door opened, and Stevens stepped out, rushing into the parking lot. James chuckled and waited until the man piled into an Escalade and pulled out of the parking lot.

The bounty hunter followed the bounty a few car-lengths back, not wanting to freak him to the point he would cause an accident. A couple of miles later Stevens pulled into the parking lot of a police station. He hopped out of his vehicle and started toward the front door.

Good boy.

James parked across the street and pulled out his phone to dial the man.

"I'm at the police station, Brownstone," Stevens answered, all but yelling. "You have to believe me!"

"Yeah, I know. Turn around and look for the black Ford truck."

The man slowly turned around. James couldn't see his expression from this far away, but his spin and sprint into the police station told the bounty hunter all he needed about Stevens' state of mind.

James pulled out his phone to skim some barbecue blogs while he waited. Stevens might have run inside and found some sort of side exit to use to escape.

A few minutes later James was in the middle of reading an article called *Nadina's Secrets of Oriceran Herbs* when his phone rang. The caller ID indicated it was Mack.

"Hey, Mack," the bounty hunter answered.

"I just got a call from the Hollywood station. They say Xander Stevens turned himself in and is practically wetting himself."

James snorted. "Pussy. All I did was make a few calls and drive by him."

"That's the power of a rep, Brownstone. Anyway, they're getting protective custody set up for him. Thanks for your help. I appreciate it."

"No problem, Mack. Talk to you later."

Well, that *shit's handled. I guess I better start getting ready for the arrival of my new friends.*

———

An hour later James pushed his way into the Leanan Sídhe.

People filled the pub as usual, their chatter fueling the happy chaos.

After a few steps, people parted and a path opened up between the front of the bar and a booth in back where James' favorite white-haired drunken fixer sat. The bounty hunter hurried toward the man, worried the Professor had already given way to Father O'Banion given how he swayed in his seat mumbling to himself. Two full mugs of beer sat in front of him.

"Thanks for agreeing to meet me," James said, sitting down across from the Professor.

The older man shot him a toothy grin. Given how red-faced he was, he probably had more alcohol than blood in his veins by that point.

"Ah, lad, good to see you. You said you had a proposal for me?" The Professor chuckled. "More little trinkets for the girl?"

"Nah. Not like that. Look, I don't want to spend a lot of time fucking around with this. The Harriken aren't done with me, so I need to get ready to deal with their shit."

"So I heard. Some rather high-end contractors are on their way to repair the group's reputation."

James narrowed his eyes. "You knew?"

"I hear a lot of things, lad. It helps when you're involved in the kinds of jobs I am." The Professor picked up a mug and took a sip. "What in particular do you need?"

"Useful artifacts for the fights I'm about to deal with. Maybe something protective."

"Not like you to worry about that kind of thing for yourself."

"Well, I'm trying to be careful for once." James shrugged. "Shay might need some protection too."

"Charity is a wonderful idea, but in the end, it's best if everyone has skin in the game. Don't you agree?"

James shrugged. "I guess. What are you getting at?"

"I have a few things that might be helpful—even better than protection artifacts."

"Like what?"

"Oh, you'll see, but if I get them for you, what do I get out of it?"

"Free muscle?"

The Professor gulped down more beer, his gaze unfocused. No, the Professor was gone. Only Father O'Banion remained. James could see the shift, see the mischief in the other man's eyes.

The bounty hunter's stomach tightened. Something bad was coming soon; he could feel it.

"'Free muscle?'" Father O'Banion echoed. "Oh, that's boring. It's easy enough to find a bounty to bribe you for an artifact job, lad."

"You want money? Jewels? What?"

Father O'Banion shook his head. "Boring. I have plenty of that sort of thing." He leaned forward to stare at James, or least try to stare with his unfocused bloodshot eyes. A huge grin broke out on his face. "I've got a much better idea. So much better."

James' blood ran cold at the hungry look in the other man's eyes. "What?"

"I've never seen you participate in the Bard of Filth Competition." Father O'Banion laughed. "And that would be a sight for anyone, I think. To see *the* James Brownstone singing lewd verses."

The bounty hunter snorted. He could tell the other man was pushing him on purpose, testing his need for the artifacts.

You like fucking with me, Smite-Williams? You're one of the few that I'd let get away with this shit. I hope you know that.

James grunted. "So I sing some dirty shit and you'll give me the artifacts?"

"Yes. Pretty fair, I think." Father O'Banion punctuated his sentence with another huge gulp of beer.

"Okay."

The older man put down his mug in surprise. "*Okay?*"

"Okay, even though it's total fucking bullshit and you know it, and only under some conditions."

"What conditions?"

"No recordings. No video, no audio; none of that bullshit."

Father O'Banion shook his head so hard his quaking body made his beer slosh over the rim of his mug. "We always record the Bard of Filth Competition. That's part of the fun, lad."

James gritted his teeth. "Then you can *not* fucking record it when I'm up."

The other man stared at him for a moment with a faint smirk on his face. He was enjoying the whole thing far too much.

"Are you going to actually try?" Father O'Banion asked. "It'll be no fun if you just mutter and grunt."

James shrugged. "I guess. What the fuck do *I* know about being a Bard of Filth?"

"It's easy, lad. Just sing a few dirty limericks. That's usually how I win."

"Dirty limericks?"

"Aye. Easy. It's just about a certain rhythm. Let me give you an example.

"There once was a man from Nantucket

"Whose dick was so long he could suck it

"He said with a grin

"While wiping his chin

"If my ear were a hole, I could fuck it."

James snorted. "This is the shit you use to win? You're fucking kidding me!"

Father O'Banion shrugged. "It's the Bard of Filth Competition, lad, not the Bard of Piety Competition. If you didn't like that one, how about this one?

"There was an old mayor of Bombay,

"Who fell asleep in his office one Sunday,

"He awoke with a scream,

"'What, another wet dream?

"This comes of not fucking since Monday."

James groaned. "Shit. This is probably the kind of thing the Harriken use to torture people."

Father O'Banion winked. "You better get to practicing your torture then. In the meantime, though, I'll see what I can scrounge up for you and Miss Carson."

The bounty hunter shot out of his seat.

"Leaving so soon?" Father O'Banion asked.

"Yeah, need to get out of here before you toss more limericks at me."

James left to the sound of the old man's laughter.

James groaned to himself as he pulled up to Zoe's house. After what he'd just gone through an hour earlier with the Professor, he wasn't sure he could handle any more intense sexual bullshit that day. The potions witch had sounded normal enough on the phone, but he could never be sure how she would behave.

After mustering his courage, James stepped out of his truck and headed toward her door. The front door opened before he even arrived. Zoe stood there in a white silk robe with a small paper bag in hand. "I've already got everything ready for you, James."

James stopped and eyed her. "You don't want me to come in?"

Zoe shook her head, a distant look in her gray eyes. "I think that's probably for the best."

James grunted. "Talk about a change."

The potions witch held out the bag with a slender hand. "Healing and energy for you as requested, blue and red bottles, and healing and energy potions for your friend as requested, green and orange." She stared at James. "This friend of yours—he's a normal human?"

James nodded and took the bag. "Yeah. Normal."

"I don't just mean not a warlock or anything. I mean not like you."

"Yeah, my friend is definitely not like me."

James saw no reason to clarify that he'd asked for the additional potions for Shay. Not everyone needed to know his business, and he was worried that mentioning another woman might set the normally flirtatious witch on edge.

"Feel free to deliver me a diamond in the future," Zoe said. "For now, though, it might best if you got going."

James frowned. "Something wrong, Zoe? You normally aren't in such a hurry to get away from me."

The witch laughed, a throaty sound. "You miss my attention?"

James shook his head. "I just want to make sure you're not in any trouble."

"No, no. No trouble." Zoe placed a hand on her chest and sighed, a faint smile on her face. "To be honest, I've been watching the news, James. I hate to say this, but I think you might be too much man for me." Her smile disappeared. "I'm interested in life, James, not death. You're surrounded by blood and violence. A woman who would want to be with you would, I think, need to be far more comfortable with death and killing than I am. I want to grow things too much to be around you."

James' face twitched, but he didn't say anything.

Zoe extended her hand. "I'll gladly be your friend and help you with your potions. Provided you continue to pay me, of course." She winked.

The bounty hunter took her hand and gave it a quick shake. "Friend is good enough. Guess I'll see you around."

"Good night, James." Zoe stepped inside and closed the door.

James lingered at the door for a moment, the witch's words running through his head.

Maybe she's right. I'm here to get potions because I'm getting ready for more killing. Who could love a man surrounded by so much death?

11

The next afternoon James went into the Black Sun. With Mack's errand finished and the bounty hunter's anti-assassin supplies either on the way or gathered, he could concentrate on preparing for the upcoming fight. At first hearing that they were coming to LA had worried him, but unlike with the bounty, he knew only a small number of people would be involved. That would make it far easier to handle without running into the wilderness or involving the Marines.

Those fuckers should have waited. Coming here's a big mistake.

Tyler looked up from the table he was clearing and narrowed his eyes. "Don't give me any shit about the number, Brownstone. I heard that Xander Stevens turned himself in, so you got what you wanted in the end." He smirked. "Can't get pissed at me for the simple pleasure I take in fucking with you."

"That's not why I'm here." James shrugged. "Don't give a shit about that."

"Then why are you ruining my day by bringing your ugly ass into my bar?"

"You made a lot of money betting on me before."

"Yeah, I did. Still sore about that? I don't fucking regret it." The bartender gestured to the corners of the room. "Also put in a security system upgrade, so if you try to beat me down I'll have all the evidence I need to take to the cops."

James snorted. "I'm not here to beat your ass, Tyler, even if you deserve it. I'm here to offer you a deal."

The bartender narrowed his eyes. "What the fuck are you talking about, Brownstone?"

"Before you said you didn't want to press your luck by starting another betting pool, but what if I told you that I could stack the odds in your favor and help make you a shit-ton of money?"

Tyler glanced around. Once he had confirmed no one else was in the bar, he moved toward James. "You mean about the killers coming for you?"

"Let's just say the repeat of Brownstone Ass-kicking Day is coming real damn soon, but this time I've got a better handle on it. A lot less highway shit will be involved." James grunted. "But all the shitholes who come through here don't need to know that."

"Why?"

Genuine confusion filled Tyler's face. James enjoyed seeing the prick off-balance.

"Why what?" the bounty hunter asked.

"Why do you want to help me? What's your angle?"

James snorted. "I don't want to help your ass. I want to help *my* ass. You're just a tool to help with that. I want twenty-five percent of the house take."

"Only twenty-five? Not fifty?"

"You probably won't agree if I ask for half."

Tyler grinned. "No, because I'm not an idiot."

"I'll also place some bets on myself anonymously. Hell, I'll put down a lot of money. That'll really get the pool going, don't you think? All those little fuckers will want a piece of the action. I'll send people this way to bet, too."

Yeah, you fuckers. You all want me to die? Well, I'm gonna survive, and I'm gonna take your money.

Tyler looked increasingly interested. "What people?"

"Lots of people, especially those who might want to bet on me living. We'll get a lot of nice back-and-forth this time from different sorts of customers, rather than just the normal garbage in this place. You probably won't get long-odds bets on my survival after last time, but if you can get a lot of people betting you'll still make a lot of money."

"Giving you twenty-five percent of the house and dealing with you winning?" Tyler walked over to the bar to slip behind it. "I don't know if I could sleep at night knowing I helped you make that much money, even if I make a lot of money too. I really, *really* fucking hate you, you know."

James laughed. "So you expect me to live? Otherwise, it seems like you'll do fine with making money and me dying."

"I think I'm beginning to wonder if betting against you is even smart. Like you said, the odds aren't going to be as great."

"Still all those house fees to be made, and lots of money from idiots placing shitty bets. Be smart about the categories, and you can easily get a lot of people to make stupid bets." James shrugged and walked over to the bar. "This might be your last chance to make money off someone trying to kill me, you know."

"How do you figure? Why can't I do this anytime you have trouble?"

James slammed a fist into his palm. "Because after I waste these fuckers and destroy the Harriken bigwigs no one's gonna bet against me again. You know I've got fan websites and shit now, right? They're calling me 'the Scourge of the Harriken.' Cops in New York recognized me on sight, and that's on the other side of the country."

"Fuck! Learning that ruined my whole week."

The bounty hunter locked eyes with the bartender, waiting in silence for the other man's inherent greed to do its work.

Tyler rubbed his chin. "Do you mind cheating a little? Maybe giving me some inside information?"

"If these assholes want to bet on me dying, I don't mind letting you know when I've taken out an assassin or two. I don't plan on dying, so I'm stacking the deck heavily in my favor with all the tools I can get my hands on."

"But what if you still get killed? From what I've heard there are some seriously dangerous assholes coming for you."

"Then I'm out the survival money, but I still want the twenty-five percent of the house take to go to a trust for someone who needs it. I'll send you the secure routing and account information."

Tyler chuckled. "Oh, you got a woman stashed away somewhere? Have to pay her to deal with that fucking ugly face of yours?"

James grunted. "Don't make me reconsider the punching."

"I've heard that money can compensate for looks, but I didn't think you were rich enough for that." Tyler barked a laugh at his joke.

Yeah, take your cheap shots, asshole. In the end, you're gonna make me a lot of money.

The bounty hunter stared at Tyler as he waited for him to calm down.

The bartender finally stopped laughing. "Why are you trusting me, Brownstone?"

"What's trust have to do with anything? If you fuck me over I'll break you in half, cameras or not."

"Can't break me in half if you're dead, asshole. I could run off to Mexico without sending shit out to whatever bitch you have hidden in—"

Tyler squeaked as James lifted him into the air by the throat and squeezed.

"Gonna make this real clear. The trust money is for someone special. I don't mind you talking shit about me, but you don't say shit about her. Fucking *ever*. If you do, I will bring the pain. Understand, fucker?"

The bartender managed a shallow nod and James let go. Tyler thudded to the floor, gasping for breath.

You're lucky I'm in a good mood, fucker.

"If I die," the bounty hunter continued, glaring down at Tyler, "and that money doesn't go to the trust, two people will come looking for you, including a killer and another person who might even be worse. Consider that my insurance policy, asshole."

Tyler sucked in a deep breath and pushed himself to his feet. He dusted his khaki pants and silk shirt with his hands before rubbing his throat. "You're a thug and an asshole, Brownstone."

"Fucking hate me all you want. I just want to know if you want to start the pool with my initial investments. I'm not gonna have time to play around with money once I start kicking ass."

Tyler flipped him off. "First, fuck you for grabbing me." He lowered his hand. "Second, when should I get the pool going?"

James smirked. "Right away. The shit starts soon, if not today or tomorrow." He turned to leave. "Send me the info and I'll transfer the money for the bets."

"None of this shit means I like you, Brownstone. If anything, I hate you more than ever."

"This isn't about you liking me. It's about both of us making money, prick."

Shay took several deep breaths as she stared at Professor Armstrong's office door. She was unsure if showing the pictures to someone else was a good idea, so she'd used software to isolate the glyphs into a separate image.

She hoped the expert opinion of an academic archaeologist might help her solve the mystery, or at least confirm her theory wasn't crazy.

It's not like the existence of the glyphs is secret. So as long as he doesn't know where I saw them it won't be a big deal.

And if it is, I can always shut him up by threatening to kill him.

Shay smiled. There were very few problems that a death threat couldn't solve.

The tomb raider knocked on the door.

"I don't have office hours today," called Professor Armstrong. "And you don't have an appointment."

"I'm not one of your students. It's Shay."

"Oh, oh. Come in."

Shay stepped into the cramped office. There was barely enough room for the desk, which was covered with stacks of papers and printed articles, as well as an ancient-looking computer.

That shit from the '20s?

Professor Armstrong, a balding middle-aged man who thought he could fool the world with a comb-over, sat behind his desk with a huge smile on his face.

He adjusted his bowtie. "It's been a long time since I've seen you, Shay. Are you still working on that book about the history of archaeology? We could go out for a drink sometime to discuss related subjects if you want. I'd be more than happy to go on record. You can quote me all you want." He waggled his eyebrows.

Shay looked down for a moment as she tried to remember the details of her lies to Professor Armstrong. "I'm still gathering notes. The publisher didn't like the direction I was going, so I'm having to do a lot of rewrites." She shrugged.

"Ah, I can understand that sort of issue. What brings

you to my office today, then, my most beautiful fan of archaeology?"

Shay barely noticed his feeble flirting; she was far more interested in his opinion on the glyphs. She pulled out two images of the glyphs and set them on the desk in front of the professor.

She cleared her throat. "I've been trying to revise my notes on ancient Oriceran and Earth connections. I found some resources that talk about these glyphs being found on different pyramids throughout the world, separated by a lot of time and distance."

Professor Armstrong picked up the images and looked between them. He shook his head. "No, this isn't right."

"Huh? What's not right?"

"Where did you get these images?"

"Someone sent them to me," Shay lied. "Claimed they had taken them in South America and Egypt."

He set the pictures down and tapped one, then the other. "They're trying to deceive you. Ignore them."

Shay narrowed her eyes. "Deceive me? How?"

"Oh, it's just... Well, you're right." The archaeologist shrugged. "These glyphs have been found on a small number of ancient pyramid structures, and they don't seem to link to any Earth civilization. The reason I'm saying these are fake is that—" he tapped one symbol, "this glyph never goes with the one right next to it. I think someone just found old images and put them together to send to you."

You would give your left nut to examine Brownstone's amulet, wouldn't you? It'd blow all your theories away. Those glyphs definitely are together on that thing.

Shay nodded slowly. "Okay, you said these symbols aren't linked to an Earth civilization. So they're Oriceran, then?"

An uncomfortable look spread over the man's face. "Look, I'll level with you. These symbols aren't linked to Oriceran either, at least not to the best of my knowledge. Now, formal academic cooperation with Oriceran scholars is still difficult at the best of times, but a number of historians and archaeologists who specialize more in that area have looked into these so-called Garfield Glyphs, and no one can link them to any existing or past Oriceran civilization."

"Then maybe there's another source. Another world?"

The professor sighed and shrugged. "There could be. There isn't strong evidence for that, but there wasn't strong evidence for Oriceran until it was basically shoved in our faces. The history and archaeology communities pretend they can explain everything in terms of Oriceran contact, but you know that just because you have a hammer doesn't mean everything's a nail. I think we academics need to face the truth that there is a lot out there we don't know." He gestured toward the window. "The only other advice I could give you is to maybe seek an Oriceran scholar and see if they can help you. Like I said, though, that can be difficult, and despite their ancient records, it's not like the average human can go over there and thumb through everything."

Shay faked a smile. "No big deal. It'll make for an interesting chapter as is. Archaeology controversies, that sort of thing. Thanks for your time."

"About that drink..."

"Drink?"

Professor Armstrong's face reddened. "I was...wondering if you'd like to go out for a drink sometime."

Shay thought back to a few of his comments during the conversation and swallowed a laugh. She'd been so focused on the information she'd not even registered he was hitting on her.

Yeah, more sad than anything, Prof. You don't have any game.

"I'm pretty busy the next few weeks," Shay replied. "Head down in research. You know how it goes."

"Oh, yeah, sure." The man sighed and looked down. "See you around, Shay."

"See you around, Professor."

Sorry, pal. Not gonna blame you for being into me, but not gonna give you any hope either.

Worrying about the construction of a new home when five world-class assassins were on their way to kill you might strike some people as an example of misplaced priorities. James, however, planned to live, and even if he died, he wanted Alison to have something to remember him by.

Curiosity was his main motivation that afternoon as he stepped out of his F-350 and surveyed the construction site. The crater had been replaced by a new foundation and new plumbing. The builders had already framed most of the house.

A skinny black man with a colored bandana hopped out

of his own F-350 and headed toward James with a huge grin.

"Hey, Trey," James called.

"Motherfucking Mr. Brownstone," the gang leader exclaimed, sticking his hand out.

James gave it a firm shake. "Everything going okay here?"

"Yeah. I'm not normally here watchin' these bitches, so you just got lucky today to be graced by my motherfuckin' presence. Don't worry, though. One of my boys always has eyes on this place. No one's gonna fuck with your new crib. These fuckers workin' hard." Trey shook his head. "I'm glad I ain't in construction. I get thirsty just watchin' 'em."

"Is the foreman onsite?"

"Yeah, that bitch Bill is here." Trey gestured to a sweaty mustached man looking through a pile of gypsum boards. "That motherfucker don't like me much, but he too chickenshit to say anythin' most of the time so we get along okay."

"I've got to talk with him."

Trey waved. "I was gonna grab some fuckin' lunch anyway. I'll have one of my boys over here in twenty minutes. You stayin' that long?"

"Yeah, should be. Thanks. Just so you know, when this shit's finished we're having a big housewarming party."

The gang leader grinned. "You may need a new house after my boys are done partyin' in it." He laughed and headed toward his truck.

James headed over toward the foreman. "Hey, Bill!"

The man looked up with a frown, but it softened when

he saw who was speaking to him. "Oh, Mr. Brownstone. Everything, uh, looking okay to you?"

"Yeah. Looks great. I guess." James shrugged. "Kind of still half a house, so hard for me to judge."

Bill wiped some sweat from his brow. "Just to make it clear, now that we've laid the foundation and started framing we're committed to the plans."

"Yeah, so? I like those plans."

"I'm just saying that with the bigger bedrooms, the additional bedroom, and the expanded kitchen, you're not going to have a lot of yard space."

James shrugged. "I don't have a dog anymore, so yard's not much of a concern."

Fucking Harriken.

Trey's F-350 roared to life and the gang leader pulled away.

Bill glared at the truck as he rumbled down the street.

James followed the man's eyes. "Problem with Trey?"

"I can't believe you'd have a gang watching your house. How can you trust criminals?"

"Hey, who better to keep criminals away than other criminals? Why, you having problems?"

Bill pointed to the gypsum boards. "Yeah, I am."

"Like?"

"There are more boards here than we ordered, and they're a higher quality material."

James laughed. "I don't see how that's a problem."

Bill furrowed his brow and blinked. "Well, it's...whatever."

The bounty hunter looked back and forth for a

moment. "So, we're committed above-ground to the layout."

"Yes. If you want to change things we'd have to add to the foundation and tear down a lot of the frame, and we'd need new plans from the architect."

"What about below-ground?"

"You want to expand the basement?"

"Among other things." James leaned closer and lowered his voice. "Let's just say I want the ability to stay in the basement a while if shit goes zombie up above, and I also want to maybe talk to you about doing something a little off the books later. An exit from the basement."

"Off the books?"

"Yeah, but with a nice premium for you and all your guys. I just don't want that shit on the official plans registered with the county."

Bill looked around as if city inspectors lurked in the shadows, ready to pounce. "I'm sure something can be arranged."

"Good. One last thing."

"What?"

"I want to upgrade the countertops."

The five killers sat around a small round wooden table in a Harriken-controlled hotel not too far from the group's headquarters. An outside observer might think they were having a friendly discussion, not deciding how to best murder a man thousands of miles away.

Trevor Moses was grateful to have a chair. All the kneeling in the Harriken headquarters was getting to his already-sore knees.

The assassin looked around the table at his temporary coworkers, amused at the cross-section of skills and humanity they represented. It'd been a long time since he'd had to coordinate with so many people.

"The way I see it," Trevor began, "it'll be better if we just decide this like professionals so we don't interfere with each other like those fools in LA did during the bounty. Not saying we should queue up or whatever, just that we should figure out in general who might go after him first."

Sabine, Connor, and Hisa nodded.

John Candle frowned. "What difference does it make?"

Trevor hadn't met the American killer before, but he'd heard of him. The man was a hothead and tended to leave a trail of collateral damage on his jobs.

The South African poison-master didn't care about innocent people getting caught in the crossfire since he didn't believe anyone was truly innocent, but he found unnecessary killing sloppy and a reflection of laziness.

You Americans are alike. Brownstone and Candle...straightforward, brave, brash, and stupid. But I can use you.

"Obviously the earlier someone goes after him," Trevor continued, "the better the chance they'll get the kill, but the longer he stays alive the worse-off he'll be, so it increases the chance someone else will take him out." He offered the others a wicked grin. "I kind of just like the idea of him getting all frantic and worried. I think I'm going to let a few of you take your shot first." He looked meaningfully at John.

Time to push him off the cliff.

"Yeah, I don't want to wait," John agreed. "I think Brownstone's got these Harriken bitches spooked because he killed a few of their idiot men. The old man's info says he's tough but not invulnerable."

Trevor shrugged. "He's got at least some magic or an artifact or something. There's being lucky, and there's killing three buildings full of men. That's not luck, and I wouldn't take him lightly."

John snorted. "I don't give a shit. That old man's info also suggests Brownstone's a straightforward kind of fuck. I don't think he'll be ready if I go at him directly. I want to take the fight to him and finish him off before he even knows what's happening. He might not even have his arti-facts on him."

"You're going to go after him in Los Angeles?"

"Yeah. I've already got tickets on a supersonic flight back to the US. I don't care what the rest of you do, but I'm not waiting around. And I'm killing him as soon as I lay eyes on him."

"You're not going to try to take him alive?" Trevor asked.

"Nope. Two million's enough, and it's been a long time since a mark's been high-profile enough to boost my rep."

Trevor raised an eyebrow and looked at the other assas-sins. Connor shrugged and Sabine and Hisa just watched, their faces blank.

"I think I'm going to stick around here, mate," Connor told John. "The asshole has too many allies in LA. He's got fuck-all to help him in Japan. I don't mind going after Brownstone, but I don't want to have to deal with the entire LAPD or the US Marine Corps. You think you can take all of them on?"

"I'm going to jump Brownstone when he's alone, so I don't give a shit about the cops or soldiers." John sneered. "And how do you know he'll come to Japan? He has no reason to leave America and the people who have his back."

Connor shook his head. "This is a guy who killed dozens of men because his dog died. He'll come. He must have his ear to the ground, and it's not like the Harriken are being quiet about hiring killers. Brownstone will come here because he'll want to end it, just like he did when he attacked the Harriken strongholds in LA."

Trevor nodded. "I agree. Besides, I'm really liking

Tokyo. Some nice booze and ass around here." He chuckled.

Connor turned to the women. "Sabine, Hisa?"

The first woman sighed. "I don't like jetlag, and I'm patient. Let Brownstone come to us. I need to collect a few more souls anyway." A hungry gleam appeared in her eyes.

Hisa gave a faint nod. "The *oni* will seek vengeance, as he has before. I will wait for him to come and make a mistake. Then I will kill him."

John pushed himself up. "Well, I have a flight to catch. Don't cry to me when you don't get any money later." He sauntered for the door, arrogance in every step.

Trevor smirked.

Thanks for wearing Brownstone down for us, John.

———

Tyler downed a shot of vodka on the rocks. He needed to be drunk to handle the self-loathing threatening to swallow him whole.

I can't do this shit. It's not like before. The fucker wants me to do it. He suggested the damned betting pool when I said I wasn't going to do another one.

The bartender poured himself another shot. Brownstone's plan had intrigued him at first, but the implications had set in after the bounty hunter departed. If Tyler worked with the man he could make a lot of money, but that meant Brownstone would also make a bunch. He'd be helping Brownstone, and not just with a minor tip on a level-one bounty.

The destruction of the bounty hunter's home had

proved that the man wasn't a god, but his defeat of the hitmen who were after him and his annihilation of the Harriken had only fed his legend.

He's just an asshole who likes to hurt people and uses bounty hunting as an excuse, and people act like I'm the criminal who should be despised?

"Fuck you, Brownstone," Tyler spat. "Fuck your sanctimonious self-righteous bullshit. Fuck your threats. Fuck your ugly face and your meathead muscles."

The bartender rubbed his neck, remembering the humiliation of gasping for breath in his own place.

I've hated the smug prick for so long. He was bad enough before, strutting around like the fucking Prince of Los Angeles, and now he's so damned cocky he thinks he can fix the betting pool against his own assassination. He's getting high on his own supply.

"Damn you, Brownstone," Tyler hissed. "Why couldn't you have just done me a solid and fucking died the last time? The money's nice, but you dying would have been better."

Tyler had spent most of his life trying to make money by the spreading and manipulation of information. It wasn't just about making a living, but proving a point to smug thugs like Brownstone—men who thought the best way to solve a problem was to punch and kick it until it went away.

Brownstone wandered around town shooting people or smashing them to the ground. They called him a bounty hunter, but he wasn't much better than a rabid animal.

Tyler, in contrast, was an evolved specimen; a man of intellect who could turn any situation to his advantage without ever threatening violence. He didn't need his fists or a gun like a certain rhino pretending to be a man.

I'm better than you, asshole. Way better than you. Smarter than you. Better-looking than you. More fashionable than you.

Tyler downed the second shot of vodka. The pleasant buzz from the first was already settling in his head.

"I am the fucking master of information," Tyler yelled to his empty bar. "And making money with gambling is all about understanding information. I'm not betraying myself by helping Brownstone with this shit. I'm *using* him. He's the fucking tool here, not me." He slammed the shot glass down.

I should have been doing bookmaking for a while. This will be the start of it. This will cement my reputation. I won't need Brownstone after this.

The bartender started laughing. In the end, it'd be Brownstone who regretted making Tyler so much money. For now, he had a lot of planning to do. People wouldn't ignore the possibility of Brownstone surviving this time, which meant Tyler needed more categories; more ways to skim profits off the gamblers.

"I'll win, Brownstone. I always fucking win in the end."

The next morning, Tyler rubbed his chin as he looked over the chalkboard and the wonderful variety of betting categories he'd thought up. He wondered if he should have invested in a wall-sized display instead of the board and set up everything electronically, but there was something satisfying about the old-fashioned approach.

He had yet to put out a major call for bettors, even if Brownstone had already sweetened the pot with his infusion of cash betting on his own survival. This round of gambling was going to make the previous event look like stupid kindergarteners trading their candy money.

Maybe I should have left the info game a long time ago and just become a bookie.

Tyler shook his head after a few seconds. Gambling didn't interest him all that much. It was the sweet rush of combining making money with the threat of James Brownstone's death that entertained him.

As if the mere thought of the man had summoned him, the bounty hunter stepped through the door and glanced around the empty bar for a moment before walking over to Tyler with a faint look of disdain.

I don't like you either, asshole, but business is business.

"Hey, Brownstone," Tyler forced out.

"I've got something for you."

Brownstone reached into his jacket and Tyler stiffened.

Fuck. I don't have a damned bounty on me. This is bullshit.

Brownstone didn't pull out his gun, but instead a small piece of paper covered in careful and neat handwriting; some sort of list. He handed it to Tyler.

"I figured this might help you set up expectations," the bounty hunter rumbled.

The bartender looked down at the paper. Five names were listed, and he read them aloud. "Trevor Moses, John Candle, Connor Malley, Hisa the *Kunoichi,* and Sabine Haas." Tyler whistled. "I'm impressed. I recognize most of the names on this list well enough to know the Harriken really want you fucking dead, and they must be paying out a lot more than a half-million to get this kind of talent." He slapped the list with his other hand. "Congratulations, Brownstone! You're moving up in the world."

"Yeah, some friends dug around a little to figure out who exactly was coming after me." Brownstone grunted. "Still gonna bet on me living? I don't give a shit either way."

"Nah, I'm still betting on you, but your instincts were spot-on in bringing this to me. This shit is perfect, Brownstone." Tyler brandished the list. "You know what this means?"

"The fucking UN of killers is coming after me?" The bounty hunter shrugged. "I'm uniting the world in my own way?"

Tyler shook his head and grinned. "It means we can get higher odds on your survival. I was worried people would all assume you would live, but with this kind of firepower coming after you, people are going to flock to the 'Brownstone Killed' bets. Plus, now we can add all sorts of bets about *who* kills you." Tyler snapped his fingers. "Video. Fly a drone around you and we can stream it on a darknet server." He rubbed his chin. "Maybe next time charge a streaming fee per head? You know, 'Pay Per View?'"

Brownstone glared at him. "Fuck you. This isn't a show, asshole. I'm not going to make this easier for these killers just to take in a little more money on the side."

Tyler sighed. "Fine. Be a bitch then. It doesn't matter. I don't like you, Brownstone, but the amount of money I'm about to make will be off the charts. You still going to call me when you take them out, right? I can really goose the bets that way."

"Yeah." The bounty hunter turned to leave. "Don't say I never did anything for you, asshole."

"Oh, Brownstone? One last thing."

"What?"

"If you want anyone to place bets over the phone, make sure they start with 'Happy Brownstone's Death Day.'"

The bounty hunter grunted. "You think you're fucking hilarious, don't you?"

Tyler tapped his head. "I don't *think* I am. I *know* I am."

This time it was Brownstone who flipped off Tyler.

"After this is all over I don't want to see your fucking face for a long time."

"Feeling's mutual, you greasy thug."

Brownstone stomped out of the bar.

The bartender couldn't stop grinning. Even in the worst-case scenario, Brownstone would die and Tyler would make a lot of money.

Somebody up there loves me after all.

Tyler frowned. "Wait. Since when is Brownstone surviving not my worst-case scenario?"

A few hours later every manner of scumbag and gambling addict filled the Black Sun, drinking, eating, and placing bets. The money was already flowing in, and none of the big action had even started yet.

Good thing I hired those temp waitresses and extra security, Tyler thought.

Excitement filled the air, even more than during the last Great Brownstone Chase, as Tyler had taken to calling the event.

The bartender finished pouring a White Russian for a gangbanger at the bar, a Demon General. The man was far from his gang's territory, and he wasn't the only gang-banger who'd traveled across the city to get a little slice of the action. Everyone wanted to get in on making money off Brownstone's death. It was hard to blame them.

The gang member took a sip of his drink. "You're not shitting us about the people coming after Brownstone, are you, Tyler?"

"From God's mouth to my ear. I'm an information broker. It's my *job* to know this kind of shit."

"They say last time you made a bunch of money off Brownstone surviving."

Tyler shrugged. "Got lucky with some hedging. Don't think he's going to make it this time with the crew he's got coming after him."

This shit's more exciting than the Sweet 16.

Despite the gathering of LA's most ethically and morally questionable people outside of the local politicians, Tyler didn't worry about trouble. As long as he kept the alcohol and the bets flowing, the fun of the event and everyone's mutual hatred of Brownstone would keep the peace.

Just in case, though, everyone had to surrender their weapons at the door, where they were placed in portable lockers he'd rented. Brownstone had suggested the idea in a text the night before, and surprisingly, no one had really pushed back.

It's like Brownstone and I are fucking business partners. Still don't know how I feel about all this, but I'll roll around in the money when it's done to make myself feel better.

Tyler chuckled, then his cell phone's ring broke him out of his thoughts.

"Hello?" Tyler answered.

"A friend of mine said you're the man to call about placing some bets on James Brownstone."

The voice was feminine but sultry. Tyler liked this woman already. Still, he couldn't risk entrapment.

"I'm just a humble bar owner, not some sort of bookie, ma'am. I think you're mistaken."

"The password is 'Happy Brownstone Ass-kicking Day'"

That's not the fucking password. Damn it, Brownstone. Guess I should have seen that coming.

Tyler heaved a sigh and considered hanging up, but money was money and the close wording of the passphrase suggested the bounty hunter fucking with him rather than a cop.

"Okay, what bets do you want to place?"

"I want to place bets against the killers, all pro-Brownstone, and then an overall bet on Brownstone, with all this over in less than two weeks. I don't want to drop physical cash."

Tyler could tell from the woman's voice she was gorgeous. Beautiful and willing to bet on a man's life; just his kind of woman.

"Sweetheart, you should come down here. It's going to be a great time. It'll be fun. I'm offering free drinks depending on how much you bet to promote the Great Brownstone Chase II, and free drinks to all the beautiful ladies who stop by."

I'm so fucking smooth.

"The Great Brownstone Chase II?" The woman let out a husky laugh. "Let's just say I'm someone who wants to remain anonymous, so not gonna stop by. Give me a crypto wallet address. I'm guessing you're smart enough to have crypto betting set up."

Tyler preferred the old-fashioned approach, but a man had to move with the times. Anonymity could be inconvenient, but it kept the cops and the feds off his ass.

"Yeah," the bartender agreed. "But I'm only accepting Trollcoin, Bitcoin, or Ether. I'll text you the address. You sure you don't want to come on down? Like I said, free drinks."

"Nah, I got better things to do than deal with a small-dick loser like you." The woman hung up, laughing.

Fucking bitch. Wonder who she is? He considered fucking with her bets, but letting personal feelings get in the way of business would destroy his hard-won reputation for professionalism among LA's underworld.

Tyler slipped his phone back into his pocket, shaking his head. Something poked at the edge of his mind, making his heart speed up as if he were missing some obvious threat. Maybe the woman's insult had hurt him more than he realized.

My dick isn't small, bitch.

The bartender looked up and realized complete silence had gripped the bar. Someone had even muted the TV, most likely one of the waitresses.

His gaze swept the bar and landed on the likely cause. Standing at the entrance was a trio of police officers, with a scowling brunette in the lead. Her name tape read HALL and her rank insignia indicated she was a lieutenant, a bit up there to be wandering around checking neighborhood bars.

The two no-neck thugs Tyler had hired for security looked at him for direction. The last thing the bartender wanted to do was agitate the police.

"Let our fine men and women in blue in so they can get a drink on the house," Tyler called, forcing a smile onto his face. "After all, they are the thin line between civilization and chaos."

The bartender was under no illusions that the local police liked him, but he had an unofficial understanding with them that as long as he kept his shit in check they would leave the Black Sun alone. A few bribes here and there were supposed to help facilitate that.

Why the fuck are they here all of sudden? They here to shut down the gambling? They didn't come during the first event. Shit.

Lieutenant Hall glared at everyone as she walked toward the bar. Now that she was closer, Tyler could make out AET on the bottom of her badge.

Why the fuck are they here? Hunting someone? But they aren't geared up.

"Good afternoon, Lieutenant Hall," Tyler said, trying for his best unconcerned voice. He nodded toward a few nearby patrons. "No enhanced threats here today, ma'am. Just normal folks, no weird magical assholes."

"Just regular assholes?" the woman said. "I haven't been in here in a while. I remember this place being more of a shithole."

Her two buddies chuckled, along with more than a few of the customers.

Fucking assholes.

Tyler shrugged. "I came into some money to do some renovations. Thanks for noticing."

"Oh? Where did this money come from?"

The bartender scratched his ear. "During, uh, James Brownstone's recent reign of terror, I found a way to monetize it."

"You mean you ran a betting pool while that trouble-making bounty hunter tore up half the county?"

Tyler shrugged. "Look, I couldn't stop the man, so I made sure I took in money whether he died or not."

Lieutenant Hall curiously looked the man up and down. "You don't like him, do you?"

"He's a fucking menace if you don't mind me saying, ma'am. Last time he was in here going after a bounty he damaged my place." Tyler pointed to the door. "Knocked my door clean off. The guy's like some sort of rabid bull, and everyone wants to drop to their knees and blow him because he takes down a few bounties here and there when we'd all be a lot safer if he were locked up in an ultramax."

The cop's face darkened and she looked at her buddies. They didn't look any happier.

Shit. Fuck it. If she wants to take me down for pissing on her hero, I can still take bets online. Tired of always hearing about fucking great James Brownstone is.

Tyler cleared his throat. "Look, why the fuck do we even have bounty hunters? What? Because of Oriceran shit and the occasional asshole who can throw some spells?" He gestured toward Lieutenant Hall. "It's not like it was twenty years ago. We've got AET now, right? You guys can handle shit. I don't care how magical some guy is, you put enough lead or grenades into him he's gonna drop dead, right?"

Lieutenant Hall's face lit up. "You're damn right! We cops are enough. Bounty hunters like Brownstone just cause trouble and destruction."

The other two nodded their agreement.

Time to press on. Now I've got her.

Tyler slammed his hand on the bar. "As far as I'm concerned, we should just let you professionals handle it rather than everyone letting some ugly thug like Brownstone run around causing property damage and risking people's lives. After all, those killers were after him. He wasn't saving us from anyone. He was saving his own ass." He leaned in and licked his lips. "Just like he is now, so you can't blame a man for wanting to make a profit off Brownstone suffering, can you?" He followed that up with a smile.

Lieutenant Hall pointed to a table where four gang members sat. "Get up. That's the cop's spot now."

"Come on," one of the gang members whined.

"You heard the lady," Tyler yelled. "Get the fuck up."

They rose and glared at Hall.

"Listen up, scumbags," the AET officer yelled. "We know what's going on here, but the LAPD has better shit to do than worry when criminals take money from other criminals. You want to bet on that asshole Brownstone dying? Be my guest. Consider this an unofficial endorsement." She pointed to herself. "Me and my friends are going to drink a little just to keep an eye on things, but as far as we're concerned this is damned *Switzerland*. Neutral ground, and we're not going to worry about anyone while they are here." She narrowed her eyes. "In exchange, you won't cause trouble, because if you do I'm going to call up all my AET friends, and we'll deliver the kind of pain that makes Brownstone's shit look like preschool." Hall dropped into her seat. "And somebody get me a damned vodka already."

Tyler chuckled and started pouring her drink. The

other customers returned to their chatting, and one of the waitresses unmuted the TV.

Cops guaranteeing the safety of my place, and AET at that? Fuck, this is turning out even better than I'd planned. Oh, Brownstone, you think you're big shit, but all you're doing is turning me into big shit. Eventually you'll be begging to kiss my ass.

14

Shay smiled at her phone when she spotted John Candle step through a boarding gate in the Tom Bradley International Terminal. The light-haired man wore a large scowl on his face and a thin jacket and jeans rumpled from his time on the plane. A briefcase rested lightly in his hands, the accessory clashing with his casual outfit.

Smuggled your guns on that easily, huh?

The tomb raider resisted the urge to go for her 9mm and open fire. A gun battle in an airport terminal filled with people would turn bloody quickly. Even if she hadn't cared about collateral damage, every traveler in the area could serve as a shield for Candle.

"Guess it's time for the plan."

Shay rose and sauntered toward Candle and the man tensed and froze.

Good instincts, asshole. Just don't go for it.

"Hey," Shay called softly. "Um, you just got off the flight from Tokyo, right?"

The assassin stared at her, his fingers twitching on the handle of the briefcase. He could probably open it and have a weapon out in seconds. She shifted the large purse she carried to conceal her weapon.

"Who's asking?" the man growled, his low voice filled with menace.

Shay shrugged. "Some guy with a weird face and a lot of tattoos gave me some money to give you a note. Well, I think it was you. He described someone who looked and was dressed just like you." She slowly held out a small hand-scrawled note on her palm, batting her eyelashes to look less threatening.

Take the bait, asshole.

Candle snatched the note from Shay with his free hand and walked away without another word. Even though she hadn't read it, she knew the exact contents:

You think you could come to my town and I wouldn't know?

I'm waiting. Come and get me. I'm just past the construction in Terminal 5.

-JB

Shay headed to a nearby coffee shop, sparing a quick glance after Candle. About fifty feet up the walkway the man's head finally dipped and he read the note. His pace picked up after that.

The tomb raider smiled, letting her previous killer instincts rise to the fore. She pulled out her phone and sent Brownstone a text.

Contestant #1 is on his way. Make him feel welcome.

Shay waited until Candle turned a corner, then hurried

into a nearby bathroom. She glanced around, but no one was inside. Her fingers went to a silver bracelet on her wrist. She wasn't sure if there were cameras in the bathroom, but it wouldn't hurt to jam them if there were.

She pulled an auburn wig from her large purse and slipped it on, followed by some oversized sunglasses. She hoisted the strap back onto her shoulder and headed toward Terminal 5.

Shay reached a row of roped stanchions and cones marking the construction zone. The foot traffic was light in the area, given that the terminal was out of use. Due to a fake message sent by Peyton, none of the workers thought they had to show up for work today. She assumed they'd figure it out before the end of the day, but the fight would be long over by then.

The woman waited for the area to clear to duck under the rope between the stanchions and hurried toward an intersection leading to a broad hallway. She pulled her gun out of the purse and slipped the extra magazines into her jacket pockets.

Shay didn't have enough ammo for a long engagement, but she'd assumed that between Brownstone and herself it'd be over damned soon.

Candle's echoing footfalls reached her ears, and she paused for a moment to take in the potential cover: commercial-sized metal garbage bins, several different stacks of wood and gypsum boards, a forklift, and pallets topped with boxes filled with moving walkway parts. The power tools that littered the ground wouldn't provide any cover, but they could trip someone.

Shay readied her weapon and waited around the

corner, keeping her breathing deep but quiet. She was waiting for her phone to buzz to signal the attack.

"You here?" Candle called. "I didn't figure you were a hide-and-seek kind of bitch, Brownstone." Something clicked and then there was a thud.

Okay, our boy is now armed.

"Wait, you thought you could sneak up on me?"

Shay's eyes widened, and she dropped, her heart thundering. A half-second later a bullet whizzed around the corner. It took a hard right turn in flight, surprising Shay even though she'd expected something like that, and flew right over her.

Reading about the man's ability didn't do justice to the bizarre sight of a bullet changing direction midflight. If she'd hadn't dropped right then she would have taken a round to the head.

Candle grunted, and she could hear him thud and roll to the ground. Several loud shots from a .45 echoed.

Shay pushed off the ground and sprinted toward the forklift, laying down fire as she turned the corner. She spotted Candle crouched behind a stack of empty pallets. The man snapped his gun back up and fired her way without even looking.

The tomb raider leapt behind the forklift as the bullet again jerked from its straight path toward her, but it struck the forklift, creating a spark and a loud *ting*.

That is fucking annoying. Damn it, Brownstone!

The bounty hunter's refusal to use the amulet against Candle was making the fight harder than it needed to be. Shay couldn't shake the feeling there was something about the artifact he hadn't told her, something that freaked him out even more than the pain involved in using it.

Shay popped up to lay down some suppressive fire near Candle. Only a quick and immediate roll after her attack saved Shay from taking a magic bullet to the shoulder.

Her heart pounded and she licked her lips.

Okay, his bullets can change direction, but it seems like they only do it once. Otherwise, the fucker would have finished me by now. Just need to keep moving. He can't see around corners, he can just shoot around them.

Her phone buzzed and she pulled it out to look at the message. Next time they'd need to set up some comm gear if they were going to coordinate attempts at clever tactics.

Fucker opened fire before I could give the signal.

Shay let out a quiet groan.

Candle sent two quick shots her way and a bullet flew over Shay and dropped straight down, jerking her phone out of her hand. Shards of plastic and glass sprayed her face.

Great. Good thing I have so many spares in the warehouse.

Shay resisted a curse or anything else that might draw the man's attention. He could obviously key in on quiet sounds somehow.

Magic is so damned annoying.

Brownstone opened up down the hall and Candle responded in kind.

Shay took a deep breath. She didn't need to hit the man, she just needed to make sure Brownstone could.

The tomb raider popped up again and fired near but not at Candle. She changed position with each shot, stepping back, forward, or to the side. Someone watching the battle might think she was doing some sort of strange dance.

Candle's bullets narrowly missed her. Only her bizarre dubstep kept her from taking a round.

Get with the program, Brownstone.

"What the—" Candle yelled.

Shay was so focused on the assassin she wasn't paying much attention to Brownstone's position. She had only a moment to register the reciprocating saw cruising through the air before it smacked into the assassin's face. He flew back with a grunt and his gun skittered across the floor.

The tomb raider didn't hesitate, just emptied the rest of her magazine into the downed assassin.

Shay changed magazines and approached the man with her gun pointed at him. A pool of blood grew beneath him and more leaked from his mouth.

"Who the fuck are you supposed to be?" Candle said between coughs. "Mrs. Brownstone?"

"For now I'm just a friend." Shay put a bullet into his head, then blew out a breath.

Brownstone jogged down the hall dodging pallets and tools. Blood matted his hair to his forehead and ran down his arm.

"You okay?" Shay asked.

"I'm fine. Nothing a few stitches or bandages can't take care of. Is he done?"

Shay looked the bounty hunter up and down, concerned about his wounds. She nodded. "Yeah, and we need to get the fuck out of here, but I'm taking a little souvenir." Shay glanced at Candle's weapon and grimaced. "Or not."

The tomb raider had hoped to grab herself a magical gun, but there was one minor issue. It was now a pool of glowing liquid.

"It fucking *melted*?" Shay slapped a hand to her forehead and nodded in the opposite direction. She'd already disabled the fire alarm on a side door. "I can't believe you threw a saw at him."

Brownstone grunted. "It got the job done, didn't it?"

Shay smirked. "It did at that. Hey, remember to give that prick a call to goose the odds."

"Tyler?"

"Yeah."

"Oh, by the way, I could tell he was pissed when I called to place my bets."

They hurried toward the fire exit. "Over the ass-kicking day thing?"

"Yep. That, and calling him a small-dicked loser."

James chuckled. "Tyler's a petty little prick, but he cares more about money than pride in the end."

Shay laughed. "You don't care that you're helping him get rich?"

Brownstone shook his head as he pushed open the fire door. "Better the Devil you know."

Maria Hall stared at the drone footage playing on her computer screen. The images weren't great given the distance of the surveillance drone from the fight, but she could clearly ID Brownstone.

No other man on this planet has a face like that asshole.

"Fucking Brownstone. You bring nothing but trouble to my town."

About the only thing good that might come out of the situation was the Caribbean cruise she'd be able to afford after winning her bets—all pro-Brownstone. The bounty hunter might be a menace, but only an idiot would bet against him at this point.

I'll enjoy the Bahamas, where I don't have to think about you.

Maria tapped the screen to halt the video, then pinched and zoomed the image. There was a woman with him, a redhead by the looks of it. Her oversized sunglasses covered most of her face, but her gun-handling skills proved she was no starlet hanging out at the airport.

"What now, Brownstone? You got a girlfriend? I don't need this Bonnie-and-Clyde shit in my town."

The AET officer picked up her phone. She had some calls to make. She needed to start looking into this woman.

James rubbed the bandage over the side of his head. Candle's little gun trick had been impressive, but better for assassination than a straight-up fight. He nodded, satisfied with the results of taking on the gun mage directly.

He glanced at Shay. The tomb raider was in the passenger seat of his F-350, hands folded in her lap and a pensive look on her face as they drove toward her Warehouse Three. She needed to gear up for the next part of their plan. After he stopped there they would head to his warehouse to grab a few trinkets, including the amulet and some explosives. Avoiding direct routes was annoying, but given the people after him security was more important than ever.

"You sure about this?" James asked.

"Yeah, Peyton's dug deep and there's nothing to suggest the others are coming to LA. Guess we don't have a choice other than to take the fight to them."

James shook his head. "That's not what I mean."

Shay looked over at him. "Look, I've got no problem with you knowing where Warehouse Three is. It's not even that I don't trust you about Warehouse Four, more that I just don't trust you to...I don't know, get greasy barbeque fingerprints on my rare books."

Why are so many people calling me greasy lately? My hands aren't greasy, and I haven't had any barbeque since yesterday.

"I'm just saying you don't have to come to Tokyo," James told her. "These guys are after me, not you."

"Fuck that, Brownstone. I'm coming. This isn't like rural Mexico. You're gonna need back-up."

"If you're sure?"

"Damn sure."

"Then let's go grab your shit."

***

With several suitcases of Shay's gear stowed safely in the back, the F-350 now hurtled down the highway toward Warehouse Two.

Does she really need five warehouses?

James grunted. Maybe she did. He only kept a small number of artifacts, but she needed a whole library and a place to potentially store large numbers of artifacts from her jobs. For all he knew, she had a warehouse filled with clothes. She had a lot more outfits than he did.

Ignoring fashion, being a bounty hunter was straight-forward. Simple, really. The scumbags he went after weren't great about keeping a low profile. Field archae-ology—tomb raiding, or whatever she wanted to call it—seemed more complicated than being a lawyer.

Shay glanced between two fake IDs she'd made with a machine at Warehouse Three, one for James and another for her.

"Still don't see why we need those," the bounty hunter rumbled.

The woman shot him a disbelieving look. "So, your brilliant plan is to fly over to Japan, the home of the Harriken and a place where four top-level assassins are still waiting to kill you, under your real name?"

"Yeah. It's simpler. It's not like I use aliases when I go down to Mexico on jobs."

Shay slipped the fake IDs into the glovebox. "Yeah, because you want the guys to be scared."

"I want these fuckers to be scared, too."

"This won't be like the Mexican wilderness. This is Tokyo, one of the largest cities in the world, and the Harriken have deep roots there. What *they* don't control the Yakuza do, and the Harriken can call on favors from them." Shay shook her finger. "And to the cops in Tokyo you'll be nothing more than another foreign bounty hunter, not some local celebrity. No, we need to play this smart, which means we don't fly into an island nation where killers are expecting us yelling at the top of our lungs that we're there."

"We could. Not like the Harriken are hiding. From what I've read, their headquarters and buildings have their gang symbol on the door. I read they even throw parties for the local neighborhoods to show their benevolence or some shit."

Shay snorted. "Harriken arrogance has gotten three buildings of theirs destroyed. Nope, we'll play this my way. At least until we've thinned out the assassins, then we'll go all Brownstone on Harriken headquarters."

"Not fond of the decoy either," the bounty hunter growled. "I'm not about risking other people's lives to protect my own."

"Calm down, there. Sure. I've got a guy on a different flight with a fake passport linked to you, but he doesn't look like you. Assassins at the level we're dealing with don't shoot random people; it leads the cops to them. They'll take one look at the guy and realize they've been fucked with. Easiest money the guy's ever made."

"You're sure?"

"Yeah, I'm sure."

"Still don't like it, but whatever. I'm still gonna have to check in with the police when we get there. What about the fake IDs then?"

"Hey, I just want to make sure they don't ambush us at the airport like we did Candle. Once we're there, if you want to start shouting from the top of Tokyo Tower, be my guest."

James grunted and lapsed into a silence that lasted several minutes.

"Something on your mind, Brownstone?" Shay asked after returned to surface streets.

"Nah, just trying to figure out how my life got so complicated."

"Isn't that what life does? Gets complicated?"

James changed lanes after checking for tails or drones. "Maybe. At least I can finally end this Harriken shit, and then...wait. Shit."

"What?"

"I better pay my rent for the next few months."

Shay gave him a sidelong glance. "I'm pretty sure it won't take us months to finish this."

"Yeah, but if I end up in some Japanese hospital after being gutted, I don't want my landlord to put my shit on the curb."

"I thought that cop liked you?"

James grunted. "Doesn't mean he's gonna provide me with free storage."

Shay laughed. "You barely have any shit anyway. It got blown up."

"I like the stuff I have."

She winced. "Sorry. Kind of a bitchy thing to say."

"You're not the one who blew up my house."

Fucking Harriken. Don't think I've forgotten about all the signed cookbooks I lost.

"Okay, okay." The tomb raider shrugged. "Next time you can just store your important crap in Warehouse One."

"Not Warehouse Three?"

Shay grinned. "Not valuable enough."

15

About half an hour later, James stepped out of the truck and eyed the strange cubicle maze dominating Warehouse Two which extruded from the small office at the side of the room. It was as if the walls had started breeding near the office.

The layout of the walls wasn't parallel, which annoyed James.

Just make a regular layout. Why is this shit so random?

A scrawny man in his early twenties emerged from the exit to the cubicle maze. He was good-looking if you liked toothpicks, James supposed.

This is the guy that Shay was willing to risk her life to save. That's got to mean something, even if he's good at computer and research shit.

"As I live and breathe," the man drawled in an exaggerated Southern accent, fanning himself with his hand. "It's *the* James Brownstone." The accent disappeared with the second sentence, replaced by vague hints of upper-class New England.

A funny guy, huh? That's almost as annoying as bounties with nicknames.

Shay gestured toward the drawler. "Brownstone, this is Peyton."

Peyton grinned. "It's kind of weird, you know, seeing the Scourge of the Harriken in the flesh. I thought you'd be taller." He held up his hands. "Not that you're not totally intimidating. I bet you look at guys and they wet themselves."

"Well, not all of them. Just a lot." James shrugged. "Soon a lot more."

The researcher laughed.

"Really, I'm just a bounty hunter who was minding his own business until those Harriken assholes had to make it personal. If they would have left well enough alone there'd be a lot more of them around. But once we take out their headquarters they won't be a problem anymore."

Fuck. At least I hope they won't. Those assholes are stubborn, I'll give them that. Hope I don't have to fly all over the world to kill every last one of them.

Peyton nodded. "Yeah, don't kick the dragon in the nose and then whine when he eats you. Totally get it." He stared at James. "Really, you're even more of a badass in person." The man nodded at Shay. "Look, she kicks a lot of ass, and you give her a major run for her money. I mean, I don't know that she's ever cleared an entire building by herself."

"I killed who I was paid to kill." Shay rolled her eyes.

"And anyway, I was there for the second Harriken raid, asshole. I killed plenty of those dicks."

Peyton shrugged. "I said 'by yourself.'"

She crossed her arms over her chest. "Whatever. I apparently try harder to make sure entire criminal organizations aren't after me. Brownstone's solution is just...a little more direct."

"Yeah, which is why you had to fake your death. Right now I bet you there are a bunch of Harriken faking their deaths because Brownstone is coming for them."

James chuckled at the idea as he stepped toward the cubicle maze. "I can't fake my death. It's too fucking complicated. It's annoying enough having to rebuild my house."

The smile disappeared from Peyton's face. "Oh, yeah. Sorry about your house."

"Don't worry. I've made them pay, and soon they'll be paying more."

Peyton pumped his fist. "Damn right. You take it to *them*, Brownstone."

Shay rolled her eyes. "I know one man's death I shouldn't have faked. Don't fanboy all over him. It's embarrassing."

"Don't worry about it, sweetheart." Peyton grinned at Shay. "I'm just showing my respect."

"Sweetheart?" Shay glared at the Peyton. "Don't make me pull a gun on you again." She glanced at James nervously.

Oh. This is the kind of guy Shay likes? Didn't expect that. Maybe I'm crowding them. Should give them a little space before I drag her off to Tokyo to kill assholes.

"Sounds like you two have some stuff to catch up on." James glanced between them. "I'm gonna look around a little if that's okay. Your warehouse is bigger than mine."

Shay smirked. "It's not the size that matters, it's how you use it. But feel free."

Once Brownstone had disappeared behind some crates at the other end of the warehouse, Shay yanked Peyton behind a cubicle wall and glared at him.

"What the fuck was that about?" she hissed.

The researcher blinked several times, his face the perfect mask of surprise. "Huh? What are you mad about now?"

"Since when do you call me 'sweetheart?'"

Peyton shrugged, the surprise on his face slipping into confusion. "I thought I was being funny."

"Did you hear anyone laughing?"

"Well, not every joke lands."

Shay groaned and stepped back. "You're gonna...give Brownstone ideas. He's gonna think we're together, the way you were talking."

Why does that thought make my heart beat faster? Fuck, I'm pathetic.

Peyton chuckled and shook his head. "Now this is something I never thought I'd see."

Shay narrowed her eyes. "What are you talking about?"

"You totally at a loss."

"Who said I'm at a loss?"

"You didn't say it. You're showing it." Peyton shrugged.

"You're smart, brave, beautiful, and can kill a man a dozen ways without a gun, but you have the relationship skills of a lump of cold oatmeal." He nodded. "Mmmhmm. It's all becoming clear to me now."

The tomb raider was too confused to respond. She blinked and wondered if a throat punch would be an over-reaction.

Okay, maybe an overreaction, but it would be fun.

Shay cleared her throat. "What's clear?"

Peyton rolled his eyes. "I'm not going to claim I'm the best guy with relationships given my almost non-existent history with women—and let's not even get into my family situation—but even my awkward and lonely self can see you are totally into Brownstone."

"That's... What? Bullshit!"

"Really eloquent response, Shay. Practically Shake-spearian." Peyton shrugged. "Nothing wrong with liking the guy. He's a badass who can bench press a sumo wrestler. The guy's got websites devoted to him, and is cool enough to have Marines help him capture hitmen. If I were going to switch teams, *I'd* go after Brownstone."

Shay's fingers twitched and it took all her self-control not to slam an elbow into her assistant's throat. "You have no fucking clue what you're talking about. No fucking clue at all."

"I'm not trying to fuck with you. I'm trying to help you."

"Help me? Really?"

The man sighed and put his hands up. "Shay, I've got your back, and that means I've got your back on your love life too. Unlike Bella and those other chicks you hang out with, I know your past, so I know when someone might work out for you. Considering we're both fake dead people, I probably understand you better than almost anyone else."

"Okay, okay. Let's talk about this." Shay looked away and took a deep breath. "Why are you so convinced I'm into Brownstone?"

"Don't you think I haven't noticed how you've been a lot nicer since you started working with him? How you break a lot fewer random dudes' fingers?"

Shay snorted. "Idiots just aren't trying to grab my ass as much. The city changed; I didn't. I'm still a hundred-percent badass bitch when I need to be."

It was Peyton's turn to snort. "Yeah, I'm sure all the horny idiot dudebros in LA spontaneously decided not to harass a beautiful woman, because they've become enlightened." He smirked. "Let's say that's true. You've also been nicer to me since you started working with Brownstone."

"*Nicer?* I tell you shut the fuck up about five times a day and I threaten to kill you at least three. I threatened to pull a gun on you earlier."

"Yeah, but it's down from ten times a day."

No, no, no. It's just me admiring Brownstone from afar and liking a few muscles here and there. I can't help it if the man obviously had an Enhance Abs spell cast on him. It's nothing more. It's nothing...

Shay sighed and slumped against the wall. "Damn it. Is it really that obvious?"

"Are these toys disguised transmitters?" Brownstone called from the other end of the warehouse.

"Just crap that was here when I bought the place," Shay yelled back.

"Oh, okay."

Shay poked Peyton's chest. "If you tell anyone I will kill you."

"Again?"

"This time the death will stick."

Peyton looked thoughtful for a moment. "Also going to give you another little tip as your helper or wingman or whatever you want to call me."

"I'm not sure I should be taking advice from you, but what the hell. I can always ignore it."

The researcher leaned closer. "Look, I'm slow when it comes to women, but it's obvious that I'm Einstein about relationships compared to Brownstone. Which is why you're doing this whole weird bashful shit instead of just taking your clothes off and boinking him."

Shay's hand went to the holster under her jacket. "I swear, if you ever use the word 'boink' again in relation to me and Brownstone I will cut you into a hundred pieces and feed half of them to some werehyena on Oriceran."

"Geeze, sensitive much? The point is, you're into him, but it's obvious to me that you're going to have to take point on this because he's clueless."

"So you don't...think he's maybe just gay?"

Peyton peeked around the wall. "It's not like I'm an expert on gaydar, but no. Why do you think he's gay? Just because he's not all over you like white on rice, Your Royal Hotness?" He chuckled. "And I thought *I* had a big ego."

Shay gritted her teeth. Beating the shit out of Peyton for seeing through her personal failings would be unfair, even by her aggressive standards.

"He...likes cooking," the tomb raider forced out. "He's

whined to me several times about the signed cookbooks he lost when his house got blown up. He lives alone. Uh, I've never seen or heard about him being with a woman."

"He's around *one* woman a lot—you. And what kind of cooking does he like?"

"Barbecue, mostly."

Peyton snort-laughed. "I don't know on what planet liking barbecue makes you gay, though I'm sure plenty of gay guys like barbecue."

"But, he, uh, went to *Wicked* with Alison."

"Oh, so, he took a girl whose is practically his daughter to a musical she might enjoy? That could make him gay, or it could, you know, just make him a good father."

Heat climbed Shay's cheeks, a sign of something she'd not felt in a long, long time: pure embarrassment.

Damn it, how the fuck did I end up in this conversation?

"My girlfriends told me he might be gay," Shay insisted. "That's he compensating with all the ultra-macho stuff."

Peyton stared at her. "Yes, the women who don't know anything about your true past or anything at all about Brownstone are totally the best people to ask for opinions on his sexuality. As far I'm concerned, if it looks like a Light Elf and sing-talks like a Light Elf, you don't say it's a Willen." He shrugged. "Look, I just think he's clueless. He's got...that feel about him. Call it man's intuition." He winked.

Shay rubbed the back of her neck. "Okay, okay. You win." She sighed. "And thanks. Glad to have someone on my side who knows everything about me and maybe, in some small pathetic way, can help me. And I know you can keep a secret."

"Glad I can help."

"That's a free 'I'll kill someone for you' card in the future, okay?" They shared a chuckle and Shay stopped first. "I'm not kidding, you know. Seriously."

Peyton raised his finger and opened his mouth, but Brownstone appeared around the corner. "We should get going soon if we want to pick up that shit from the Professor."

Shay shot a meaningful glance at Peyton before nodding to the bounty hunter. "Okay, let's roll."

16

Two hours later James was sitting on Shay's surprisingly comfortable leather couch, checking through the Japanese National Police Agency Bounty Awareness app on his phone. The English offered by the translation options could have been a little better, but all the main points were there for him to search for good ass-kicking candidates.

James and Shay had booked tickets for an early morning supersonic flight from LAX to Narita, which would get them into Tokyo by early afternoon. Even on a supersonic plane, the flight was a little longer than James would have preferred.

"If man was supposed to fly, God would have given us wings," the bounty hunter muttered.

Fuck. Next time I start a war against a gang, better make sure they are based out of Des Moines or something. Original Gangster Disciples of Corn or some shit.

The stairs creaked under Shay's steps as she went down

to the first floor. "So your decoy is on the way, and he's packing my perfect fake ID. That should stir up our remaining assassins."

James only offered a quiet grunt in response.

Shay glanced down at his phone. "Reading anything interesting?"

"Looking for some high-level bounties." James held up the phone. "If I commit to three level-four or higher bounties we can ship our weapons legally, and then we don't have to worry about extra bullshit."

"We're flying in under fake IDs?"

"I can use a 'registered agent' to commit to the bounties it says. So I'll just use the fake me as the registered agent."

Shay sighed, a faint look of disappointment on her face. "Having you around is occasionally a good thing, I guess."

James chuckled. "We're going to Japan because of me."

"True. Don't get a big head about it." Shay shrugged. "What's the big deal? I smuggle stuff internationally all the time. In some ways it's easier when you're going from a place like here to Japan, because they are expecting less of it than when I go to and come back from Mexico."

"Why smuggle when we don't need to? Besides, the last thing I need is some Japanese AET team busting down my hotel door with some fancy exoskeleton suit or whatever."

Shay smirked. "They aren't called AET there. I'll spare you the Japanese, but they are TEK units. You're right, though. They do have fancy exoskeletons."

"Whatever. Same difference. AET hates my ass in LA, and the only reason they haven't come after me is because other LA cops have my back. I don't have a Sergeant Mack in Tokyo."

Shay furrowed her brow. "So let me get this straight... We're flying halfway across the world to take on four high-level assassins, and after that we're planning to storm Harriken headquarters and kill every single motherfucker there, but you're not worried about any of that. You're worried about the *cops*?"

James shrugged. "The point is, no reason to do it illegally if I can find us a way to do it legally. Illegal shit complicates everything, and this situation is complicated enough as it is."

The tomb raider shook her head. "Sometimes keeping stuff simple in the short-term makes it more complicated in the long-term. Maybe that's something you should start seriously thinking about."

James swiped the phone screen, narrowing his eyes at one of the bounties. "I never wanted any of this. I just wanted to do my job and be left alone with my dog."

"You sure about that?"

James looked up from his phone with a frown. "What are you getting at? You saying this shit is my fault?"

Shay made her way to the couch and dropped onto the opposite end, then placed a hand on James' shoulder. "Look, Brownstone, I'm just saying... If you wanted a low-profile job that didn't bring trouble you would have been an accountant, not a bounty hunter. Especially not a high-end bounty hunter going after some of the toughest assholes out there."

"I didn'—" The bounty hunter shut his mouth at the touch of Shay's finger.

"I'm not blaming you for those Harriken pieces of shit or going after them for killing your dog. I helped you against my better judgment because I thought it was a dick move on their part. I'm just saying you have to face the reality that your life is not gonna be simple if you're taking on necromancers and international criminal gangs. Sometimes just kicking ass isn't enough. I wish it were." Shay shrugged.

James grunted, tension suffusing his neck and shoulders. He didn't have a good response to that. It wasn't like Shay was wrong, but it wasn't like he was going to quit and take up gardening.

Is this about Father Thomas? About wanting to protect people? Or is that just bullshit?

A feeling he couldn't describe burned in the back of his mind. Using his strength to help others felt deeper than just being a product of his childhood experiences. It was like he was doing what he had always been meant to do.

Nah. That's the shit everyone tells themselves to justify their crap. I'm not special just because I can kick more ass.

James decided the best strategy for the moment would be to push the conversation back toward something more comfortable.

"We don't have to smuggle," the bounty hunter rumbled, "because I've already found three bounties that should work. I'll have to check in with the police on arrival to get the permits and officially they'll all be for me, so don't get caught by the cops. They take gun possession very seriously over there."

Shay rolled her eyes. "I've been to Japan more than a few times. Have you?"

James shrugged. "I've watched movies and read books set in Japan. I'm not totally clueless."

The tomb raider laughed. "Brownstone, don't ever change."

———

Trevor folded his hands on the table in front of him as his gaze traveled between the other three remaining assassins.

And here I was half-worried that John would kill Brownstone and get all the money.

"I have to say," the man began, "I thought John would give a more impressive performance."

"Are you sure about the information you received, mate?" Connor asked. He stared at the tapered silver wand he was rolling between his palms. "Maybe the American cops are just trying to cover for Brownstone. They're practically bloody blowing him in LA, from what I've heard."

Trevor shook his head. "Even though there's no video of the fight I could get my hands on, I've got video of the crime scene. Candle's the only dead one there, very little blood that's not his. I'm not even sure if he hurt Brownstone."

"I respect John for going first, even if Brownstone killed him. At least it gives us some proof that Brownstone's reputation isn't total shit."

Trevor arched an eyebrow. "You think the Harriken would drop that much money on rumors?"

"We've all run into men who get lucky. Just saying these gangs get superstitious and easy to spook."

"That's some major luck," Hisa murmured. "And what about the bounty action against the LA Harriken?"

"I don't trust that the cops didn't just kill a bunch of the bastards and get Brownstone to agree it was him."

Trevor shook his head. "That's a pretty impressive conspiracy theory, Connor."

The other man snorted. "Conspiracy theory? Those bloody Oricerans had been fucking around with Earth for thousands of years, but anytime people mentioned faeries or aliens people laughed at them. You had people trying to hide the truth. You never know what you can believe anymore, mate."

Trevor resisted laughing at the other man. Being stable wasn't a requisite for being a good assassin. If anything it could make it harder.

"Just saying," Connor mumbled. "Doesn't matter. The Harriken are going to pay out for Brownstone dead or alive, so someone will need to supply him."

Trevor nodded. "That still leaves us asking what our next move should be. I think us agreeing on who might go is still a good plan."

The gathered assassins all nodded and murmured their agreement.

A good plan for me. I've checked this man out. Most of you have no chance of winning. You don't fight a tornado by throwing another tornado at it. This will require tactics and patience.

"We could go after him together." Connor looked around the table. "Not my favorite idea, but tossing it out there to you for due consideration, my highly esteemed colleagues." He grinned.

You're almost as annoying as John, although in a different way, you English prick.

"And split the money?" Trevor chuckled. "Not interested. I wouldn't have flown across the world to meet with the Harriken for a lesser amount. Splitting the money would make for a lesser amount."

"I'm not interested in working with any of you either," Hisa told them. Today she'd shed her Japanese appearance and was now a blonde-haired emerald-eyed woman in a business suit.

Trevor noticed that her slight Japanese accent still came through in her voice. Maybe that was why she tended to prefer Japanese disguises. The faintest hint of something out of place could help someone see through a disguise.

"I'm not here to share the money," Sabine agreed. "And I'm willing to wait until one of you wears him down. Besides, the fewer assassins left in this world, the less competition we all have."

"Ah, you don't even care if I live or die?" Connor asked with a smirk. "And here I thought we had a real connection, *Fraulein* Haas. I was going to ask you out after this was all over."

Sabine rolled her eyes at Connor's poor attempt at German and his behavior. "I'd prefer that you died, or at least that you don't defeat Brownstone before I do."

The man puffed out his chest. "Just because Brownstone killed some glorified gun boy doesn't mean he'll win against me."

"He's won against a lot of wizards."

"Yeah, because *he* was going after *them*, not the other way around." Connor waved his wand with a flourish. "The tough ones always underestimate electricity. It's not just

167

about wearing more armor or using a skin-hardening spell."

Trevor nodded. "Are you going next, then?"

"Yeah. Why the bloody hell not? Brownstone might be tough, but I doubt he's immune to a good shock. It'll make it easier to capture him too, and why take less money when there's more on the table, right?"

"The bastard is arrogant. I can't believe he's flying straight into Japan under his own name. Since he ambushed John at the airport he knows we're after him, and now he's coming straight at us." Trevor rubbed his chin. "Though I doubt he knows all of our abilities. We can still use that against him."

Don't have to win in a straight-up fight with him. That's where all these idiots will go wrong—except maybe Hisa. I have to go before her. Connor or Sabine might weaken him enough to put him in a hospital. Then it'd be an easy kill.

Trevor resisted the urge to glance at Hisa. He might have to arrange for her death soon enough.

"After what happened in LA," Connor stated, "the man probably thinks he's untouchable. I've taken out a lot of guys like that. It'll be easy enough to stun his ass and drag him back to the Harriken, then I'll take a long vacation with all that money." He winked at Sabine. "You can come along on the vacation if you want."

The woman muttered something in German before switching back to English. "You're a fool if you think you can take him alive. If you want to have any chance of getting paid you should plan on killing him."

Connor stood and started tapping his wand in the palm

of his hand. "Do you want to go next instead? Ladies first, is that it?"

The woman sneered and waved a hand dismissively. "I will kill Brownstone when the time is right. If you're so eager to die, be my guest."

Connor sneered. "Yeah, thought so. This is the kind of job that needs some balls. I've got a mighty fine pair I'd love to show you."

Sabine leaned back in her chair and ran a finger over the polished obsidian pendant she wore around her neck. "So many men have died at my hand. Their balls didn't save them." A feral grin appeared on her face.

"You *threatening* me, woman?" All the humor drained from Connor's face.

Trevor looked at the two, his face impassive. If they wanted to kill each other he wouldn't intervene. Sabine was right about one thing; it'd be less competition.

"I kill no one without the promise of payment," the woman declared in a cold voice.

Connor slipped his wand into a holder under his jacket. "Yeah, thought so." He waved to the gathered assassins. "I wouldn't bother figuring out who's going to try after me, mates. Brownstone's going to be bloody dead very soon."

The electricity wizard strutted toward the door.

Trevor smirked.

I bet Brownstone kills you quicker than he killed John.

17

"Please place your thumb on the DNA scanner, Mr. Brownstone," the Japanese cop said, his English slightly accented but still near-perfect—and a hell of a lot better than James' near-complete lack of Japanese. "Your registered agent Mr. Capelli submitted the paperwork before your arrival."

If I'm gonna be traveling the world kicking ass I need to start studying more languages. Maybe Shay could help me.

James placed his thumb on the panel, then a faint burning sensation struck his digit. He removed his thumb and shook it out.

The bounty hunter glanced over his shoulder. Shay was waiting on a bench in the hallway in front of the police kiosk.

Shay talks all her shit, but in the end she has my back even when she's not next to me.

The bounty hunter blinked a few times, letting the thought settle over him. He relied on his confessor to take care of his soul, but otherwise he'd tried to live his life not relying on anyone else. He'd convinced himself that he was protecting both his simple lifestyle and the people who might get caught up in violence.

Everything had changed. He was about to adopt a teen girl, he was living in Mack's rental apartment, and now Shay was helping him with both information and jobs. For that matter, he had a business arrangement with that prick Tyler.

Life was anything but simple anymore, but the idea of having friends and people he could rely on didn't bother him like it once had.

James returned his attention to the police officer processing his temporary foreign bounty-hunter license. He had to admire the efficiency of the whole operation. The minute he'd stepped off the plane he had been directed to find the nearest police kiosk.

The cop looked up from his screen. "The scan checks out. Now I have to ask you a series of questions."

"Go ahead."

"Have you familiarized yourself with Japanese laws concerning bounty hunting, Mr. Brownstone?"

"Yeah. I read all the notices and documents in the app on the phone."

"Do you understand that non-bounty deaths will be prosecuted as murder?"

James nodded. "Yes. Same in America."

"Do you understand that your temporary bounty-hunting license extends only to bounties that have been issued by the National Police Agency of Japan and no other criminals, officially reported or otherwise?"

"I do."

The cop cleared his throat. "This doesn't mean you should stand by if a crime is occurring, but we don't want you to hunt random criminals."

"Gotcha."

"Let us continue. Have you declared all dangerous weapons, artifacts, and beings of interest, including those that would be classified as either magical or technological? Please note this includes non-sapient magical creatures."

"I have."

For a brief moment, James felt a twinge of guilt. Despite his big speech to Shay, he'd not declared his amulet as an artifact, nor the toys he'd borrowed from the Professor. Then again, smuggling artifacts remained far easier than smuggling weapons, since the authorities in most countries didn't have a reliable and widespread way of easily detecting magical violations.

From what James understood, before magic spilled back into the world in a big way it was easy for certain people to keep track of what was going on. Now magical forces were just part of the background noise.

The cop nodded. "Policy dictates that I make it clear that we take a much dimmer view of collateral property damage than many other countries, especially America. You will be responsible for payment to the affected individuals in addition to fines."

James resisted the urge to laugh. The Japanese would have to fine him a shitload before they caught up to the fines the LAPD and the City of Los Angeles had slapped on him during his last adventure.

"I'll keep that in mind," the bounty hunter assured the policeman.

"Please note, severe damage to the wilderness will be fined and potentially prosecuted."

James nodded and managed not to grunt in annoyance. His first bounty *did* involve a forest, but it wasn't like he was planning to burn it down to smoke out the bounty. He couldn't help but wonder if something like that had happened.

"I always try to keep damage to a minimum."

Well, at least damage to innocent people's shit.

The cop narrowed his eyes. "You have a reputation, Mr. Brownstone. Don't think we're not aware here of how much damage you can do, and of some of your more destructive incidents in Los Angeles. Also be aware there are no outstanding organizational bounties on the Harriken in Japan."

"Who said anything about the Harriken? I'm here for the three bounties I committed to." James forced a smile. "I've always wanted to visit Japan, so I figured I'd pay for my trip by taking out some scumbags for you while I'm here."

The cop's face twitched and he nodded. "I see."

"I totally love Japanese culture." James grinned. "Really interested in things like *Masamune* swords and *kintsugi.*"

Total surprise settled over the cop's face for a few seconds, then he smiled. Everything about his body language changed, including his shoulders relaxing.

Glad those Harriken assholes gave me some shit to work with. Now, this guy doesn't think I'm just an ignorant asshole foreigner here to make trouble, even if I kind of am.

The cop tapped at his keyboard at a furious pace for about thirty seconds before offering a slight bow to James. "Enjoy Japan, Mr. Brownstone." He reached into a drawer beneath the counter and pulled out a thin card with an embedded chip. "This is your temporary bounty-hunter license. Please do not lose it. That may cause complications." The man looked to the side for a moment before looking back at James. "Also be aware that the law in Japan states that if a TEK team arrives you will submit to them immediately, otherwise they may be forced to treat you as hostile." He frowned. "Excuse my use of the abbreviation. They are our anti-magic police."

"Yeah, I know about them." James took the card from the police officer. "Thanks for your help." He turned to leave.

Self-defense still applies. I can't help it if I have to kill everyone who shoots at me at Harriken headquarters.

James lay on the hotel bed, head resting in his linked hands. Shay stepped into his room and closed the door.

"I finished the sweep of my room. No weird shit in there."

The bounty hunter grunted. "No reason for there to be. All those assassins have probably bugged the decoy's room, and his hotel is about an hour away."

"Given everything that cop said to you, I think the plan we discussed before is our best bet."

James sat up, frowning. "So you go after these assassins while I take the easy way out?"

Shay laughed. "Brownstone, you're the only man in the world who would think taking on a bunch of high-level bounties while acting as bait is 'the easy way out.'" She leaned against the closed door and crossed her arms. "And we've talked about this already. You're a great bounty hunter. Great instincts. I'm a field archaeologist now but I was a killer before, so I have better instincts when it comes to professional hits. Plus these assholes don't know about me, so I have the element of surprise."

"These aren't exactly normal assassins."

Shay's smile vanished. "I'm not exactly a normal woman. I've taken on my share of people with magic." She raised a hand. "Look, no one loves my life more than I do. I'm careful—more careful than you—so if anything, this plan is far safer."

James grunted. He still didn't like the idea, but he understood Shay's logic. "You really think this will work?"

"They're gonna figure out your decoy fast if they haven't already, and now your name is in the police system. If they don't have access to that the Harriken do, so it's only a matter of time before they figure out what you've done and come for you. But we're already here and set up, plus we've got this hotel under fake names so they can't easily trace us here."

"Sure hope you're a good enough killer to take out these others."

Shay rolled her eyes and snorted. "They aren't killers. They're assassins."

"Same thing."

"Is a Chevy the same thing as a Ford? You might as well

sell that antique of yours and buy any old random truck, right?"

James gritted his teeth. That was a low blow.

"No."

Triumph spread over Shay's face. "Always remember, killers are killers and assassins are pussies."

After traveling for the whole day he was finally settled, and James decided he didn't want to go after the bounty until the following morning. It'd give his body time to adjust.

He'd better send Alison a text so she knew what was up.

James pulled out his phone and tapped out his message.

Safe in Tokyo with your aunt. Going after a legit but weird bounty tomorrow morning. Tell you about it when I get back.

It was pretty early in the morning in Virginia so he didn't expect a response, but that didn't stop his phone from chiming.

Be careful.

When am I not?

All the time. A rolling eye emoji followed.

Okay, talk to you later, kid.

Love you, Dad.

James just stared down at the phone. His reason for coming to Japan was encapsulated in that three-word message. The Harriken stood between him and a happy future with the people he cared about.

"Fuck you, assholes. You had your chance to leave me alone. It's my turn."

18

"I can see why they call this place 'the Sea of Trees,'" James mumbled as he made his way through the dense cypresses and Japanese red pines. The omnipresent buzz of cicadas prevented a silent approach.

The occasional flutter of a bird or scuttle of some small ground animal kept the bounty hunter focused. After all, he wasn't there for a leisurely stroll.

I think I prefer the desert. Fewer places for bastards to hide.

James' phone buzzed and he pulled it out to check the text from Shay.

I'm back about a hundred yards and keeping pace. By the way, I fucking hate that coat.

James glanced over his shoulder. Shay was behind him, but he couldn't see her. Still, knowing she had his back allowed him to focus on the bounty.

He smirked about the coat. He'd purchased several of the same style of gray coat she'd hated during their trip to Mexico. It was functional when it came to hiding weapons and allowed good range of motion. Not only that, he'd gotten a sweet deal. Plus, it amused him to tweak Shay over her strange fashion obsession when it came to him.

Some branches crunched under his boots as he headed toward the last known sighting of his bounty.

It was hard for him to think of it as a bounty since this was his first true monster hunt, and a nice level-five at that.

Magic's return and the stronger connection to Oriceran might have flooded the world with assholes like King Pyro or allowed gangsters to wield magic swords, but it'd also revealed another horrible truth: monsters were real and more than ready to prey upon mankind.

An unusual spike in suicides, even for an area already known for it and believed to be haunted, had led the authorities to investigate, and that had led to drone confirmation of a so-called "despair bug."

The name didn't do justice to the huge monster. Oriceran reports indicated they had similar creatures in some of their forests, but no one was sure if that meant they'd traveled to Oriceran from Earth or the opposite.

"Come out, you overgrown maggot," James shouted. "I don't want a waste of lot time in a place where I can't easily see the fucking lines of fire."

Another ten minutes of hiking brought him even deeper into the forest. He could tell he was getting closer now to his prey. The trees and bushes grew increasingly brown, their leaves withered and dying. Their very life force was being sucked out.

James halted and frowned. The dying vegetation wasn't the only change. Since he'd entered the forest he'd heard bugs or animals, but now only the quiet moaning of the wind and the crunch of branches under his feet were the only noises.

"Yeah, bet you're real close, aren't you?" the bounty hunter murmured. He reached up and tapped the amulet resting underneath his shirt. He'd used a metal piece to separate it from his chest, and he wasn't sure if he would need it.

James unholstered his .45 and held it with both hands. If even the insects were scared, the despair bug was damned close.

He continued moving deeper into the forest, hoping that Shay still had visual contact. The one wildcard in the situation was the despair bug's ability to get into people's heads. From what he'd read, it only worked on people who already had issues with depression or sadness. The mere possibility of the ability's use kept the regular police away from the area, though.

"You're not so tough, are you, asshole?" James shouted. "That's why you have to hide and play mind games. Why don't you just come out and fucking deal with me?"

A wave of vertigo struck James and he stopped, shaking his head and trying to regain his balance. The sensation vanished.

What the fuck was that?

"You shouldn't have come here, James," a man called.

The bounty hunter spun, gun raised. No monster or Japanese hiker stood in his line of fire, but instead an American priest in full vestments. It'd been years since he'd seen the man, but he still recognized the smiling face of Father Thomas.

"You're not real," James declared and shook his head again. The priest had died protecting him. That was what he remembered, but the more he thought about it the more confused he became.

"I'm *very* real, James, and I'm sorry. I failed you."

"No, you... Fuck, this isn't right."

Father Thomas laughed. "My ward is a foul-mouthed thug who kills people for a living." He laughed. "And then you inflict your grievous sins on Father McCartney. I wonder how he feels at night, having to help you cleanse your disgusting demon-tainted soul."

Vertigo struck James again. "It's...not...like that."

The priest snorted. "It's not? Aren't you here to murder hundreds of people? *How* is it not like that?"

James rubbed his forehead, trying to focus. "You don't understand. I've tried to get them to leave me alone, but they won't fucking stop."

"He who lives by the sword dies by the sword!" the priest thundered. "You make up these excuses, but you crave blood and violence, all the while using some demon amulet." He pointed at James. "Your soul is already lost, you pathetic evil man."

"That's not how it works," James argued. He rubbed his eyes and tried not to trip over his own feet.

Father Thomas didn't seem to be standing in one place. He disappeared and reappeared every few seconds.

"This is just bullshit," James said. "It's all bullshit."

"Bullshit? No, it's the truth. Why do you think I kept that horrible thing from you? It whispers to you, doesn't it? Whispers dark things in a language you don't understand.

Demon speech. Satan's promise of power in exchange for a soul."

"Fuck you, you piece of shit. You're not real."

Father Thomas sighed. "How long do you think you can last, James? How long before that demon corrupts you? It's already corrupted your soul. Next it'll take your mind and you'll kill everyone you care about. Shay, Alison...they'll all die at your hands, but there's a way you can save them. There's still a chance for you to protect the ones you care about."

James blinked several times, trying to focus on the priest. The man seemed to have stopped teleporting and now stood about three yards away.

"Save them?" the bounty hunter mumbled.

"If you're not around them to hurt them they'll be safe, but we have to be certain you'll never come back. That there won't be a risk." A sick smile covered the man's face. "You know what you have to do, don't you, James? Take that gun, put it in your mouth, and pull the trigger. Save those you love from your demon-tainted soul. Save the *world* from your demon-tainted soul. You've used something evil and it's too late for you."

He's right. I don't even want *to use the damned amulet. How many times have I asked myself what the price of using it is?*

"Do it, James!" Father Thomas shouted. "Be a real man for once instead of a demon puppet. You think they'll understand when you finally turn on them? You think you'll be able to control yourself? You won't. You made a mistake even telling Shay about the amulet. You know that in your heart. You know she'll soon learn what a disgusting demon freak you are and leave you. Maybe she'll try to kill you to stop you before it's too late, but you'll kill her first." He sneered.

"Shut up." Increasing vertigo made it hard for James to stand.

"Maybe the girl will be your first victim. She can see the truth, you know."

That's right, Alison can. "I told you to shut up. You're not Father Thomas."

"You think because she's told you about your beautiful soul it's true? She's just scared. She's hoping to gain enough magic at the school to save you, but it won't be enough. You'll kill her with your bare hands as that demon amulet screams in your mind."

"Shut the fuck up!" James roared. He glared at the man, breathing ragged.

The priest clucked his tongue. "You already know what you have to do. Kill yourself before it's too late."

James' phone buzzed and he shook his head, confused. A couple of seconds passed before he pulled it out of his pocket and looked down at the text.

Who are you yelling at? From what I can see, you're shouting at nothing.

Hands shaking, James texted back.

Don't worry about it. Just having a little discussion with my bounty.

The bounty hunter slipped his phone back into his pocket and narrowed his eyes at Father Thomas.

"How fucking *dare* you take his image," the bounty hunter snarled. "Of all people! I will destroy you."

"You're a monster, James. A freak. Look at what you can do. Look at your *face*. Demon-tainted monster. You think you can have a family? You think a *thing* like you should even *have* a family?" Father Thomas laughed. "The only thing you should seek is oblivion."

"How fucking dare you do this to all those people," James yelled. "You piece-of-shit monster. You've been killing innocent people and feeding off them by driving them to suicide."

"I'm not the monster, James. You are. There's only one way out. One solution for a demon-tainted monster like yourself. If you want to save the ones you love, kill yourself. Do it. *Do it!*"

James whipped up his .45 and squeezed the trigger three times, but Father Thomas didn't jerk back, fall down, bleed, or otherwise react. Instead, he faded slowly from sight and the lingering vertigo stopped.

"Nice try, fucker," the bounty hunter shouted. "Now you've gone and made this personal. Very fucking personal. I'm gonna enjoy this."

Chitters echoed all around James and he spun, gun raised. He spotted something twining around a tree trunk.

Six pairs of jointed legs were evenly spaced down its long segmented chitinous body. Fully extended, it would easily measure over ten feet. Massive mandibles jutted from its mouth. The alien horror was completed by something mundane but more disturbing by the juxtaposition: a triangle of large human eyes above the mandibles. All three stared at James.

The despair bug screeched and launched itself from the tree.

James leapt to the side to dodge the monster.

"Die, you ugly son of a bitch." He opened up with his

pistol, its loud report echoing in the forest.

Each bullet that struck the carapace bounced off, not so much as scratching the creature. The bounty hunter emptied his entire clip as he backed away.

The despair bug let out another eerie hollow chitter and rounded on James, its mandibles snapping.

The bounty hunter grunted. "Guess that's why you're a level-five."

James holstered his gun, yanked a throwing knife from underneath his coat, and threw it at the despair bug. It bounced off to no effect. He'd not hoped for much, but when dealing with magical creatures a man could never be sure what might work.

The despair bug charged again and James rolled to the side, narrowly missing impalement by one of its razor-sharp legs.

James pulled out another knife, this time a heavy saw-toothed blade. He rushed toward the still-turning bug and brought down the knife with as much force as he could manage.

If it were a man the bounty hunter could have easily shoved the knife clean through, but the carapace again deflected the blow like it was thick steel armor.

Come on, you could at least fucking bleed for me?

The despair bug whipped up the back of its segmented body, sending James smashing into a nearby tree trunk.

James grunted and pushed himself off the tree, his back aching. He grabbed the fallen knife.

The despair bug's three eyes remained focused on him. The creature didn't charge him, but instead screeched loudly.

That your native version of talking shit? Fuck you.

James let out a quiet grunt as an idea occurred to him. He roared and charged the despair bug and the monster launched itself at him, but at the last second the bounty hunter spun to the side to avoid the pincer grasp of the mandibles.

With both hands he again brought down his knife, but this time right into the top eye of the creature. The blade sank to the hilt into the creature's head and it thrashed, knocking James to the side.

Blue ichor spewed from the wound, and the despair bug continued whipping back and forth. James pulled out another knife and shoved it deep into another eye, and the thrashing intensified.

James locked his legs around what passed for the head and yanked out his .45, and reloaded it, all the while being bucked by the monster as if he were participating in the world's most horrific rodeo.

The bounty hunter shoved the barrel into the remaining eye and kept pulling the trigger until the despair bug collapsed to the ground. It continued to twitch for a good half-minute before it finally stopped moving.

James hopped off the dead monster and looked down at his ichor-stained coat and pants. "Yeah, that's fucking disgusting."

Connor loved going after marks he respected. Frying some poor sucker who wouldn't have a chance against him was for pussies. Sure, he'd take the money, but he loved the idea of taking down someone who might have a ghost of a chance.

He wasn't sure how much he had believed in Brownstone before, but seeing the bounty hunter lay waste to the strange monster made Connor a fan. The assassin almost regretted having to turn the man over to the Harriken.

Sorry I have to take you down, Brownstone. If it wasn't for the money I'd take you out for a beer, because that was badass.

The assassin fished his wand out and raised it. He estimated the distance at about sixty yards, which normally wouldn't have been an issue.

Too many bloody trees. I'll need to get closer.

Connor hated being in the creepy-ass forest, but once he'd realized where Brownstone was going he'd figured it'd be the perfect opportunity to take the man down.

Just my luck I'll probably run into a ghost who'll kill my ass before I can get to Brownstone.

A shadow passed over him from behind. Connor's heart rate kicked up and he spun, wand at the ready. Agony shot through his wrist as a blade pierced it and he hissed in pain as he tried to go for his gun with his left hand.

The knife was pulled out of his wrist and was in his other arm in flash. His attacker shoved a knee into his stomach and Connor collapsed to the ground.

Through the haze of pain and adrenaline, Connor realized his attacker wasn't a ghost but a beautiful dark-haired woman.

"Wait... Are you some sort of Japanese ghost who takes the appearance of a sexy woman?"

"No, idiot. I'm all too alive."

Fuck. Of all the people to take me out, it has to be a bloody hot babe? Damn it. Or, fuck, did that bitch Hisa decide to remove some of the competition?

The woman put a knife to his throat.

"Which one are you?" the woman asked, her voice low.

The woman's accent was American, which meant she wasn't Hisa in disguise.

"I'm just a tourist," Connor said, wincing in pain. "I got lost. You have to believe me."

"A tourist carrying around a wand?"

"Wizards go on vacation too, you know."

The woman chuckled and pressed the knife lightly against this throat, drawing blood. "I'm gonna ask again, and if you don't tell me the truth I will kill you. Which assassin are you?"

The woman was obviously a pro. Maybe he could deal with the situation a different way.

"Connor Malley. Come on, you don't have to do this. What's this about? You mad 'cause the Harriken didn't hire you to take out Brownstone?" He hissed in pain. With the adrenaline starting to fade, the burning in his wrist and arm dominated his attention.

The woman's face twitched. "I'm asking the fucking questions here. You're some sort of electrical wizard, right?"

"Yeah. Listen, we can work together. Harriken didn't do an open call, but you can work with me and still make some money." He sucked in a breath and tried to ignore the pain. "We take down Brownstone, and I'll split the money with you. Fifty-fifty, right down the middle. Sounds fair, right? Hell, sixty-forty."

If the bitch would just get off him he could down a

healing potion and end his pain.

"There're three more, though, right? Three more assassins? Hisa, Sabine Haas, and Trevor Moses?"

"You're well-informed. Come on, we can do this together."

"Where are the others?"

Connor had to admire the woman's instincts. Her gaze never left him, not for a moment.

"We're doing this individually, but we had an agreement about the order." Connor took several deep breaths. "Who are you?"

Fuck this hurts.

"My name is Shay Carson. I'll probably meet you someday in hell. No hard feelings." She slit his throat.

James finished taking pictures of the downed despair bug with his phone and uploaded them. He waited for a few minutes for confirmation that the pictures would be acceptable proof of the kill. Dragging some ten-foot long weird-ass monster out of the middle of the forest was about the last thing he wanted to do.

Fuck, I don't even want to carry that thing's head. And the smell. Damn!

His phone buzzed.

Photographic evidence received and confirmed. Please stop by any Tokyo Metropolitan Police Department Station for your reward.

They followed with a smiling emoji face wearing a police hat.

His phone buzzed again.

Hey, get over here. I've got a present for you.

James looked around until he spotted Shay waving through the trees. He made his way through the forest toward her, and once he spotted the body he picked up the pace.

"See?" Shay exclaimed. "It was a good plan. This is...*was,* Assassin Number Two. Meet Connor Malley. Before he joined his victims, he kindly informed me that the assassins aren't going to attack you together. That's gonna make this shit easy. We can pick them off one by one."

James grunted. "Guess that's good news."

Shay sniffed. "Geeze, Brownstone. I think that's the worst shit I've smelled in a while. And what was all that yelling about earlier?"

The bounty hunter looked away. "The thing got into my head a little. They don't call it a 'despair bug' because it's funny."

"You okay?"

Fuck. No. Maybe it's time I actually trusted her for real.

"Yeah." James rubbed the back of his neck. "When it was fucking with me, it made me think about some stuff about the amulet. Some stuff I haven't told you yet."

Shay narrowed her eyes as she wiped off her bloody knife on Connor's body. "What?"

Maybe I am a freak or a monster, but I need to go forward with this shit and find out the truth.

"The amulet," James began. "When I wear it, it whispers in my mind."

Shay shrugged. "Okay, what does it whisper?"

James stared at the woman. He'd been expecting her to

be shocked or disturbed or at least a little surprised, but instead it was like she already knew what he was going to say.

"I don't understand the language," James said. "I don't even know if it's a real language or if that's just how it sounds in my head."

"Pay more attention. Concentrate. Maybe you can grab some sort of clue that'll help me." Shay stepped toward him and tapped his chest where the amulet lay underneath his shirt. "We can figure this shit out, Brownstone. We just need to collect more evidence."

"Do you have any leads?"

An uncertain look descended over the tomb raider's face. "I'm still doing a lot of research. I'll let you know when I have anything." She blew out a breath. "For now, let's get the fuck out of this forest."

"Sounds good to me."

Shay turned to leave and James fell in behind her. He was happy to have taken down the monster, but he couldn't help but feel she was hiding something from him.

Fuck that noise. That's just the despair bug's after-effects. Shay's killed more than a few times to help me, so the least I can do is believe in her.

James glanced over his shoulder at the deceased Connor Malley. "Worried about anyone finding his body?"

Shay held up a gloved hand. "No prints, and once they run his DNA and realize who he is I think they'll stop looking, especially given where we are."

"Okay." James stared down the body. "Sounds good."

He smiled to himself. Next time he would handle the body better.

Shay waited across the street from the Tokyo police station while Brownstone collected his money. She didn't understand why the tech-loving Japanese, of all people, insisted that someone show up in person so they could initiate an electronic money transfer.

The sun hung low in the sky, and it wouldn't be that much longer until night fell. Then again, night never truly fell in Tokyo—one of the few cities on the planet that could make New York look like it lacked sufficient lighting.

The tomb raider continued to watch the flow of humanity walking up and down the street and thought about the impact of the return of magic. Twenty years before Japan had been one of the safest countries on Earth, with crime rates so low the police had begun obsessing over the most trivial of crimes to justify their existence.

The return of magic had hit the safe country harder than other, rougher countries. Maybe the ancient magic ran deeper in the island nation for good or bad, leading to a dangerous concentration of magical criminals and monsters.

After a good thirty minutes of people-watching, Shay narrowed her eyes and ducked into a nearby alley. She had almost missed it.

Every few minutes a Japanese woman passed by the police station and looked toward the entrance, first a young woman wearing a low-cut black dress and matching tights, then an elderly woman, then a policewoman, and then another young woman, but this time in a pantsuit.

By the time pantsuit woman went by, Shay realized what small detail had been poking at her from the edge of her subconsciousness. The women were all wearing the exact same ankle-high black boots.

Could mean nothing. Maybe it's just a popular brand here.

Shay pulled out her phone and dialed Brownstone.

"I'm almost done," he rumbled.

"I'm pretty sure I've got eyes on Hisa," Shay murmured.

"She's not gonna kill me in front of a police station. That'd be fucking stupid."

"No, but she'll follow you and waste you when you're not paying attention. If I'm right, she keeps changing her appearance except for her boots for some reason."

"Maybe she really just likes the look of the boots. You're the one obsessed with fashion."

"Huh? I'm not obsessed with fashion."

"You bitch about my coats all the time!"

"Hating those ugly-ass things isn't the same as being obsessed with fashion." Shay sighed. "It doesn't matter. Anyway, focus on the boots. Because she can change her appearance, we might not get eyes on her before an attack.

You should go into the bathroom and put on the amulet just to be safe."

Brownstone grunted. "I don't need the amulet. From what you told me she's not super strong or anything. She can just use the illusion magic."

"If she shoves an ice pick through your brain you'll die, Brownstone. Stop bitching about your whispering-doom necklace and use it to make sure we take this bitch down."

"Okay, okay."

"Thank you. I've got a plan. When you come out, go to your right. About five blocks down there's a subway entrance. Go down there. Make sure you look for a suspicious-acting Japanese woman with ankle-length black boots."

"What else is she wearing?"

"Could be anything, remember? She's probably not gonna keep the same appearance."

"Good point."

Shay rolled her eyes. "I'll jam the cameras once the action starts, but we're not gonna have a lot of time. Anyway, once you spot her, keep her busy."

"Keep her busy until what?"

"You'll see."

When he stepped out of the police station James was still awed by the amount of paperwork the Japanese police had made him fill out to claim his bounty. He'd assumed after they accepted a phone picture of the dead despair bug that collecting his payment wouldn't be a big deal, but the gauntlet of forms had seemed like it would never end.

He stifled a yawn and made his way down the street. At least he'd get a little action soon to get his blood pumping.

Been a busy day. Killed a despair monster, and now we're about to finish off the third assassin.

The amulet whispered in the recesses of James' mind. He tried to concentrate on what language was being spoken. He began to wonder if it was just sending sensations to his brain rather than speaking a language.

Guess that shit's not important right now. Do your worst, amulet. After the fucking bullshit with the despair bug, you don't seem so bad.

James' heavy booted steps echoed on the stairs leading to the subway.

Too many damned people crowded the subway platform; if a fight broke out there somebody innocent would be hurt. A few people glanced his way, but no one wore suspicious boots.

The bounty hunter looked up and down the platform and started walking toward an area where there were fewer people. The ocean of humanity became a lake and then a puddle, and in the end, he found a lonely stack of crates next to a wall.

Yeah, this will work.

A few moments later light footsteps sounded behind James and he turned around. An attractive young Japanese woman in a leather jacket, white t-shirt with what looked like an angry cartoon rhino, and jeans stood behind him smiling. She'd accessorized with ankle boots. She ran her fingers along the hem of her jacket.

The boots combined with her sudden appearance left James no doubt as to her identity.

Should have tried to take a shot, Hisa.

"I saw you on the street," the woman told him. "I love your sense of fashion, since it matches mine." She offered him a playful grin. "I want to show you something I think you'll appreciate."

James grunted. "What's that?"

Her hands trailed up the side of her legs, then underneath her jacket until they arrived at the hem of her shirt. "I'm not wearing a bra."

The bounty hunter bit back a groan. He was almost embarrassed for the assassin.

Didn't these assholes do any research on me? She seriously thinks that shit's gonna work?

The woman whipped her shirt up, exposing herself, and James sighed in response. Then there was a *click* and she kicked at his leg. A knife protruded from the tip of the boot. It slammed against James' leg and snapped off, clanging to the asphalt.

The woman frowned and leapt back, adopting a defensive stance. "You've been poisoned, Brownstone-*san*. You'll be in agony in seconds. I considered trying to take you alive, but after you emerged from the forest unharmed by Connor I knew you were too dangerous."

James shrugged and cracked his knuckles. "I'm no doctor, but I'm guessing you have to actually get that shit into my blood for it to work and that weak-ass kick wasn't enough. Sorry, Hisa. That's who you are, right? Hisa the *Kunoichi*?"

"Yes. You deserve to know the name of the woman who will take your life."

Hisa spun around to deliver a roundhouse kick to his head. James grunted and only moved about an inch.

The assassin launched a series of quick strikes, and James blocked them with little effort but didn't counterattack. Without enhanced strength, a normal person couldn't generate enough force to injure him when he wore the amulet.

And people say I'm the one with the attitude problem. Just wandering the streets and people show up to kill me.

Hisa followed up with a flurry of kicks, punches, and sweeps. James either blocked them or moved out of the way. Frustration continued to build on the woman's face.

"You see, you didn't have to do this," James remarked. "I just mind my own fucking business, but people keep trying to kill me. It's really fucking annoying. And don't you dare feed me some bullshit line about how it's nothing personal."

"Death is *always* personal." Her breathing ragged, Hisa stepped back to glare at James. "Why won't you fight me? You think a Japanese person is unworthy to take your life?"

James snorted. "One of the few guys to get a decent hit on me lately was Japanese. I don't give a shit where you were born when it comes to ass-kicking."

"What then? You disrespect me because I'm a woman?"

Out of the corner of his eye, James spotted Shay creeping around a corner toward Hisa. The bounty hunter kept his gaze focused on the Japanese woman. If he shifted his eyes it might tip off the assassin.

"I don't care about sex either when it comes to ass-kicking. It's a brave new fucking world, and everyone can kick ass with the right magic."

"Then why won't you fight me?" Hisa tried to slam her fist into his neck, but he blocked.

James chuckled and stepped back. "You bitch way too much for someone who is supposed to be a pro."

Shay continued moving toward Hisa, her face a mask of concentration.

"Your arrogance will be your end, James Brownstone. Enough disrespect." Hisa reached into her jacket to pull out a pistol. "Now you die."

Shay whipped out a knife and stabbed Hisa in the back. "He's not disrespecting you, bitch. He's respecting me."

The assassin collapsed to the ground, coughing blood. She turned her head, her eyes wide, to stare up at Shay. "No, it can't be! You're dead!"

Shay winked. "Like I told someone else, it didn't stick."

The Japanese assassin smiled, surprising James. Her head lolled to the side, and her breathing stopped, then her body shimmered for a moment and the young attractive woman was replaced by an older and plainer woman in shorts, a tank top, and boots.

"Good call on the amulet," James said. He pointed to the boot with the broken blade. "Poison knife. Not sure I would have been able to take it."

He'd had no plan to purposefully test his poison resistance anytime soon. He still didn't understand the nature of the amulet's protection.

Shay pointed to the crates. "We could put her body behind there. No one will find her for a while."

James reached into his pocket and pulled out a small

brush with white bristles. Glyphs decorated the handle. "I've got a better idea."

"What, you're gonna paint her? Not exactly the time to get into disturbing hobbies."

"No, watch this. It's an artifact the Professor loaned me. I asked for some protective stuff, but he thought this would be more helpful."

The bounty hunter knelt by the body, then sucked in a breath and dipped the brush in the still-spreading pool of blood. His hand made careful movements as he drew a glyph on the corpse's forehead.

"Okay, Brownstone, you're officially creeping me out," Shay muttered.

"This shit better work in English. The Professor said it would." James took another deep breath. "Too far, too near. Too empty, too full. Too living, too dead. Dispose. Dispose. Dispose."

Don't make me regret this, Professor.

A flat and opaque black circle appeared over the body like a hole in the fabric of reality.

James blinked. "Huh. Didn't expect that."

He couldn't spot any texture or patterns. It was like looking into a part of the world God forgot to paint. Light didn't penetrate it.

"What the fuck is that?" Shay exclaimed.

The hole doubled in size and. James jerked back and scooted away.

You could have explained that part, Professor.

Droplets of blood started rising into the hole to be swallowed. The perfect darkness didn't change. Hisa's hair flowed up, pulled up by the silent force of the hole. A few seconds later, the whole body jerked up and disappeared in an instant.

James' stomach knotted.

You said I didn't need to turn this shit off, Professor. I hope I didn't just start the destruction of Japan.

"Brownstone, do we need to run for our lives about now?" Shay asked, uncertainty underlying her tone.

"It's okay...I think."

"You think?" Shay said. "You don't fucking know?"

Oh, fuck. Did I accidentally just end the world?

The hole winked out of existence. The apocalypse was over before it started.

James scrubbed a hand over his face and let out a sigh of relief.

Shay poked at the air where the hole had been. "Where does that dump her? Staten Island? Bermuda Triangle? Atlantis?"

The bounty hunter chuckled. "Nah. The Professor explained it to me. There's...this kind of world in between. I don't quite understand it all, but it's not Oriceran or here. You can send shit there but you can't get it back."

Shay nodded. "I've read a little about it. It's the last resort for some Oriceran banishments and shit like that. Perfect way to clean up a body." She laughed. "So we're filling the void or whatever with our trash and bodies?"

"Something like that. Just, with the Japanese being more uptight, he thought this might help. I figured we didn't need it in the forest because we were in the middle of nowhere."

"Yeah. And how did you convince the Professor to loan you something like that?"

James grunted. He thought about lying, but Shay would find out eventually.

"I have to participate in a bullshit dirty limerick competition."

"One of those Bard of Filth things?"

"Yeah."

Shay burst out laughing. "Oh, I can't wait to see the video. That shit will go viral in two seconds."

James tried to burn a hole through her head with a glare. "I made it fucking clear there's not gonna be anybody taping that shit. I'll burn down the entire Leanan Sídhe before I let anyone record me."

"I guess I'll need to make sure I'm in the country that night then. Once in a lifetime and all that."

James shrugged. "Whatever. Let's just go get something to eat. I want something in my stomach before the next asshole comes to kill me."

Shay smiled as she plopped the sauced beef slice into her mouth with her chopsticks. "Sure, it's not *your* kind of barbecue, but yakiniku is close."

The way Brownstone gobbled his meat suggested he liked it well enough, or at least that he was hungry, though the sight of the muscled and squared-jawed bounty hunter stabbing his meat with a fork in a restaurant filled with slender Japanese businessmen amused Shay.

Brownstone swallowed. "It's not Jessie Rae's, but it's not bad. The Japanese know their way around seasoning meat, I'll give them that."

Shay rose and dusted her hands on her pants. "I have to go hit the ladies' room. Try and not get killed while I'm gone."

"Sure."

The field archaeologist smiled and headed down a short hall. She glanced back and forth, and after confirming no one was there she pulled out her phone.

It was still ass-early in Virginia, but Shay had made certain promises to Alison—even if Brownstone didn't know about them.

The teen answered on the second ring. "Is he all right?" she whispered.

"He's fine. We've already taken out three of the five, and then there's the headquarters."

"But that's just normal guys, like before in LA?"

"Yeah, for the most part."

Alison sighed at the other end. "Will it be over after this?"

"The problem with running a big criminal gang is that other people are always ready to stab you for your position. Once we take out the headquarters, I'm sure all sorts of groups will move in and finish off the remaining Harriken."

"But those are just more bad guys, right?"

"Yeah, but those bad guys don't have a grudge against Brownstone."

"Just...keep him safe."

Shay wished she could give the girl a hug.

"He's fine, sweetheart, and I won't let anything happen to him."

20

James sat on the edge of the hotel bed feeling pretty damned satisfied. He'd done a little pest control, and two more of the assassins were down.

The bounty hunter had worried that the assassins would play it safer than the hitmen who'd come after him in LA during the Harriken's previous attempt to take him down, but now the trip to Japan was looking like it'd last days instead of weeks.

Shay linked her hands and stretched her arms over her head. "Almost time for the big show. Maybe you shouldn't even bother with the other bounties. Killing that fucked-up monster is more than enough service."

"Nah," James replied, pulling his phone out of his pocket and bringing up the bounty app. "I definitely want to go after the next guy."

"The serial killer?"

The bounty hunter nodded.

Shay shook her head. "You don't know anything about

him, other than it's a Japanese guy in his early twenties. Shocker. They're not exactly rare in Tokyo."

"He's not just some random killer. He's using magic to paralyze people somehow, then the fucker disembowels them while they are still alive." James' face tightened. "At least that despair bug has the excuse of a parasite who feeds on humans. This is just a man who tossed away his humanity." He curled his free hand into a fist. "I *want* this fucker."

"And how long do you intend to spend running around a foreign country trying to find a serial killer? You're not a detective, Brownstone, you're a bounty hunter."

James grunted. "Reach out to Peyton and have him narrow shit down. Break into the police computers if he needs to."

Shay snickered. "Not like I'd have to tell him to do that. Then what? If it were that easy the cops would have found him ages ago."

"We don't *have* to find him. Not with my plan."

"Huh? How the hell do you figure?"

James stared down at the victim list on his phone. "Have Peyton start spreading rumors electronically, and I'm gonna spread a little money around on ads. The cops are being tight-lipped, but once Peyton confirms the general hunting grounds for the fucker I will run some local ads talking about how I'm coming for him and calling out his manhood—that sort of shit."

Shay frowned. "I don't know. Wouldn't that drive him deeper underground?"

"Nope. From what I've read, this asshole's been picking up the pace the more the media talks about him. He also left some sort of note ranting about the corruption of society, and how anyone who is helping fight the chaos is a tool of darkness and shit like that."

"Huh." Shay shrugged. "Guess I shouldn't be surprised that a serial killer would be fucked up. What about the Harriken?"

"What about them? It's not like they don't know I'm here. The assassins might have been distracted by the decoy, but three of them have found me. No, those Harriken fuckers aren't gonna come after me on the street. I'm past the point of fucking hiding."

Shay shrugged. "Okay, then. I guess let's smoke ourselves out a serial killer."

———

Trevor looked out the window into the brightly lit streets of Tokyo, watching the lines of lights marking the traffic. "It's down to just us, Sabine. Hisa missed her check-in."

The German assassin glanced down at her necklace. "I want to go last."

Trevor turned away from the door to smile at the woman. "You sure? Now that Brownstone is making so much noise trying to rattle some serial killer it's easy to track him. I'm going to kill him very soon, you know."

Sabine shook her head. "No. You'll try to, but you'll fail."

"I'm not an idiot like the others. I've no intention of taking him on directly. I've also been persuaded he's dangerous. He'll never see the face of his killer."

Sabine's smile mocked him. "A coward will never kill

Brownstone, only a warrior like him." She licked her lips. "And that warrior's soul will be mine soon."

Trevor snorted. "I don't care if you think I'm a coward. I'm an assassin." He headed toward the door. "And Brownstone is just another mark."

A few days passed while James taunted the killer with the help of Peyton, Shay, and various public-awareness ads.

Currently James sat across from Shay at a cracked and scratched wooden table at a yakiniku place in Kabukichō. Several prostitutes dined nearby, shooting him bright smiles occasionally. A few tattooed Yakuza watched him as well with a mix of wariness and respect in their eyes. None dared approach him.

Peyton's research and hacking of police records revealed the killer was almost exclusively targeting people in that neighborhood, which was dangerous anyway. The researcher had also discovered the police had concealed that the killer had slain more people than had been revealed to the media, including several prostitutes in the area.

The local Yakuza were hunting the man and the rumors said that even the Harriken had a kill-on sight-order if anyone encountered the culprit, even though in general they kept a light touch on the area.

James hadn't seen a single Harriken, which made him wonder if they were purposely avoiding him.

Yeah, you fuckers aren't so tough now, are you?

"I can't believe so many websites and radio stations are

running those ads," Shay said, glancing down at a picture of James' face next to brightly-colored Japanese characters. "It's like you're some weird celebrity who came over to hawk soap or something. 'Buy this. Brownstone says it's the only thing stronger than him!'"

James chuckled. "Hey, there's nothing bad about the ads. They just talk about my track record and how I'm gonna protect the people of Tokyo. It's more like a political ad than a soap ad."

"Brownstone for mayor of Tokyo. He'll beat down taxes like he beats down criminals!" Shay laughed. "I just...can't get over you sometimes. Assassins target you, so you go straight to them. You're looking for a serial killer, so you take out ads bragging about yourself while sitting in the heart of the city ruled by your enemies."

The corners of James' mouth quirked in a smile. "It's sim—"

"Simpler," Shay finished for him. "Yeah, yeah. You're lucky you're such a badass, Brownstone. Most other people would have ended up dead long ago pulling half the shit you do."

"I've gotta be me." James grinned.

Shay rose and winked. "You keep being you. I'm gonna make myself scarce in case our boy won't approach unless you're alone. Enjoy the rest of your meat." Her mouth quirked into a smirk.

Probably thinking something dirty again, aren't you?

James picked up a slice of beef with his fork. "I will." He stuffed it into his mouth, then flagged down a server to order more beef and pork.

When Shay departed relief spread over the faces of

several of the prostitutes who had been watching the pair. A few batted their eyelashes at James.

Not here for that, ladies.

The bounty hunter planned to spend a full hour or two at the restaurant, just as he'd done the last few days, and with the amount of food he'd ordered the owner didn't mind. He'd even taken a picture of James making a V sign and put it on the wall.

James had trouble understanding the man and the translation app on his phone didn't help much, but the owner seemed to think the bounty hunter brought him good luck. Or maybe the owner just believed the bounty hunter would kick the ass of anyone who might cause trouble.

A few minutes later James' phone buzzed and he read Shay's text.

Whatever you do, don't eat anything else that comes out. Encountered another friend of yours.

James grunted. He was almost out of beef. Fucking assassin should have waited until after lunch.

A thin man in a rumpled business suit and glasses pushed into the restaurant, his gaze focused like a laser on James.

The bounty hunter locked eyes with him. He didn't need Alison's soul sight to see the evil radiating from the shifty-eyed bastard.

The new arrival marched right over to James' table and inhaled deeply. "You're James Brownstone, right?"

"Yeah." The bounty hunter frowned, surprised at the man's crystal-clear words and British accent.

Huh. Guess it doesn't make any sense for him to have an American accent if he's gonna speak perfect English.

"What's *your* name, asshole?" James rumbled.

The man sniffed. "You can call me 'the Cleaner.'"

Of course—another nickname.

James glanced at a nearby table with several Yakuza. He nodded to them and then to the door, hoping they understood his meaning. The men offered polite nods back and rose, rattling off something in curt Japanese to the other customers.

Soon, a conga line of gangsters, prostitutes, and middle-aged men was making its way outside.

The owner frowned and started shouting something in Japanese, but the Yakuza shouted back. The owner looked at James.

"I'll pay for their meals." He pointed at the Cleaner. "And get some beef slices for my new friend."

"Yes, Brownstone-*san*," the owner replied and hurried to the back.

The Cleaner continued watching James, resting his elbows on the table and his chin in his hands. "You sent those maggots away to save them? It's not worth your time. None of them deserve to live."

"It's less trouble for me if they're fewer people around, so it doesn't matter if they deserve it."

"I think you and I are alike, Mr. Brownstone."

James snorted. "Not fucking likely."

The Cleaner smirked. "Aren't we? You're a cleaner too. Scum infests your country and your city and you get rid of it. Sometimes you even kill, don't you? How is that different than me?"

"I only go after legal bounties, not random-ass people." James narrowed his eyes. "And I don't torture them."

"Random? There's no randomness to any of this. I target those who are poisoning my society and I kill them. Whores weaken the moral fabric of society. Corrupt businessmen sell out our country's soul for profit, and people who talk at the movies are rude and care only about themselves."

James blinked. "People who talk at movies?"

"Rude is one of the worst things a person can be. It proves they don't care about anyone but themselves. Antisocial behavior should be punished."

The bounty hunter sighed and shrugged. "Look, I don't really give a fuck about your reasons. You've killed, and the cops want to talk to you. You have two choices: you can either turn yourself in or I can take you in. I'm not gonna lie—I'd love to smack you around a little, you twisted fuck."

The Cleaner slammed his hand on the table, causing James' utensils to clatter. "I will *never* surrender to the tools of corruption. I would rather die first."

"Not my call, but either way you're going in."

The Cleaner laughed and shook his head. "You think you're strong and can defeat me." The man pulled off his jacket and ripped open his sleeve, a glowing tattoo of a *tengu*, a winged Japanese long-nosed goblin.

"Nice ink. I am supposed to be impressed?"

"You shouldn't have sent the others away. With this I can stop anyone, even the mighty James Brownstone."

James resisted pulling his gun out and ending the fucker right there. The only reason he didn't was that the poor owner would have to clean up all the gore.

"If you're helping out Tokyo so much," the bounty hunter said, "why not tell people about it at your trial?"

The Cleaner snorted. "The law is a tool of the corrupt system. I will never get a real trial. Most people have let the darkness swallow their minds."

The owner pushed through the door leading to the back, two plates filled with beef slices in hand. He hurried over to the table and set a plate in front of James and one before the Cleaner. He shot a pleading look at the bounty hunter.

"Don't worry," James said. "I'm not gonna break anything in here. I like the food too much."

The owner nodded, bowed, and scurried back into the kitchen.

The Cleaner snatched up a piece of beef with his chopsticks and downed it without much in the way of chewing.

"You should savor the flavor, asshole," James commented. "Otherwise, why even bother going out to eat?"

"Food is a distraction. Flesh is a distraction. The corruption has blinded us all to that. The existence of Oriceran only confirms that we're in the Latter Day of the Law. This world is degenerate and suffering. I will embrace the darkness to push back the darkness, even at the cost of myself. That is how much I am willing to sacrifice despite the cesspool called civil—"

The Cleaner dropped face first into his plate of beef slices.

James stared at the man, waiting for him to pop up and continue his rant.

A scream ripped through the alley behind the bar, and

seconds later Shay burst through the kitchen door and rushed to the table.

The tomb raider stared down at the Cleaner. "It's fucking poisoned. I spotted Trevor Moses sneaking into the kitchen and adding a special ingredient. I thought I told you not to eat anything."

James nodded at the Cleaner. "I didn't eat anything. The asshole did."

"Whatever. Grab him and let's go. I was hoping we could zap Trevor's body to the World In Between, but they've already found it."

"Damn, now I won't be able to come back to this place. At least I can take out some trash for them."

James fished several large bills out of his wallet and tossed them on the table, then threw the Cleaner's still-warm body over his shoulder and headed toward the door.

Shay followed him. "Four down, one to go."

Tyler groaned and slowly opened his eyes. Something was buzzing.

"What the fuck?"

It was his phone.

The bartender/information broker snatched the phone from his nightstand.

"Some fucker better be dead to be calling me so fucking early."

He rubbed his eyes and looked down at the text.

Four out of five gone, TM most recent. Only SH left.

Tyler bolted upright, now awake. "Time to update the odds." He texted back.

Cops playing too. Real family-friendly event. It's almost respectable.

Cops?

Yeah, an AET chick and some of her friends.

Brownstone waited a good minute before responding.

Is she betting on me?

Yeah. She's like me. She hates your ass, but likes money more.

That's me. Bringing people together.

Fuck you, Brownstone.

Tyler followed his text with ten middle-finger emojis.

The next morning, James had just finished his shower when his phone rang. He slapped a towel around his waist and headed over to the grab the phone.

Unknown number.

"This is Brownstone," the bounty hunter answered.

"This is Sabine Haas. You've come to Japan to look for me. I thought I would save you the trouble."

James couldn't help but chuckle. "You assholes are calling me directly now? You've got balls."

"It's my understanding, Mr. Brownstone, that you prefer direct confrontation. Now that you have disposed of the others, I'm ready to deal with you. In thirty minutes I will be at a construction site. I will send you the address. If you wish to end this, come for me there."

"I could just call a TEK team to come and bust your ass. Not even sure there's a bounty on you. Not really worth my time."

Sabine gave a throaty laugh. "If you call the police I'll

escape. I'll wait until the next time you're sitting at some cute little restaurant surrounded by your sycophants and we'll start the battle there. If you're not a coward who would hide behind the weak, you'll come to the construction site."

"*You're* the fucking coward, bitch."

"Perhaps, but you can prove you're not one. Also, don't bother having your little girlfriend try to sneak up on me. I suppose I shouldn't have been surprised to learn she was still alive. She was always a roach, but if she's so eager to kill she should join you and face me."

James grunted. "I don't know what you're talking about."

"Fine. I don't care. I can kill her later, after I've killed you. Come to the address in thirty minutes. *Auf wiedersehen.*" Sabine hung up.

The phone buzzed, signaling the text with the address. James glanced at the address and activated his map app.

"Damn it."

James wouldn't have enough time to get breakfast first.

Fucking inconsiderate assassin.

James and Shay rolled up to the construction site. Tall stacks of metal girders and wood littered the area, and a few massive cranes and bulldozers had been parked at the edge of the zone. Construction had barely begun, with only a few water pipes laid in recently-dug ditches.

Shay surveyed the site and pointed into the distance.

Sabine was about a hundred yards away on top of a stack of wood.

"Everything I've heard and that Peyton could dig up suggests she's gonna be tougher than the rest."

"Let's just get this shit over with so I can get some damned breakfast," James rumbled.

Shay laughed. "Love your priorities there, Brownstone."

Eerie whispers sounded in his mind.

Yeah, you're gonna help me today, amulet.

James had bonded with the amulet before they'd gotten in the car. Sabine might be tough and have a magic necklace, but he figured that only meant she'd last a couple of minutes longer than her buddies had. He hadn't even bothered to bring either of his healing potions. He wanted to save them for the Harriken raid.

This shit won't take long. She's got a nickname, and she's calling up to taunt me? She hasn't met anyone like me before, and I'm gonna punish her for fucking with people's souls.

The bounty hunter and the tomb raider stepped out of their rental Toyota, their coats flapping in the light breeze as they made their way toward the assassin.

Sabine hopped off her makeshift throne and sauntered toward them like they were all meeting for brunch. Her jeans, tennis shoes, and cream-colored top only reinforced the casual feeling of the encounter. They stopped about ten yards from each other.

The German assassin smiled. She had something approaching happiness in her icy-blue eyes. "Thank you for not making this more complicated, Mr. Brownstone. I appreciate your bravery and honor it."

"Hey, I like shit simple. This was simple."

Sabine's gaze cut to Shay. "And look at you! I'm sure I can squeeze some money out of someone for killing you. Well, killing you again."

Shay snorted. "You have to win first, bitch."

The assassin chuckled and returned her attention to James. "You should be honored, Mr. Brownstone. I've decided you're worth a rare display of my true power."

James shrugged. "Thanks, I guess."

The whispers grew louder and more insistent in his mind as if the amulet was worried about something.

Sabine's pale fingers rubbed the polished obsidian pendant hanging from her necklace. "*Grendel, gib mir deine Stärke. Grendel, mach mir die Krallen deiner Rache.*" The necklace glowed for a few seconds and the woman's eyes turned solid black.

James grunted and whipped out his .45. "What the fuck did she just say?"

Can't the Harriken just stick to hiring people who speak Spanish or English to kill me? I'm an American. We don't do foreign languages.

Shay frowned. "She asked Grendel to give her strength and make her his revenge claws."

"I thought the Grendel was just a monster in a story."

Shay pulled out her 9mm. "Guess not. Fucking magic."

"Fucking magic," James echoed.

Sabine laughed, her eyes as dark as the hole to the World in Between. "Magic has returned. True strength has returned. Now I will show you my power."

James narrowed his eyes, realizing for the first time that Sabine didn't have a gun or any obvious weapon. She hadn't worn a coat, so she didn't have anywhere to hide one. What that implicated about her strength wasn't lost on him.

"Let's end this quick." James pulled the trigger of his gun.

The brains of the Claws of Grendel's Vengeance didn't splatter all over the dirt and rock behind her. She just rubbed the side of her face. "That hurt."

James grunted. "It wasn't supposed to hurt. It was supposed to kill you."

Sabine charged James, spinning and launching a kick at him. He squeezed off another shot as she connected with his chest, sending him flying twenty feet back. He slammed into a pile of steel girders and his pistol flew from his hand.

Shay ran to the side and squeezed off round after round, but her bullets didn't hurt the assassin any more than James' had.

James shook his head and pushed off from the metal, a little sore from the blow. "Nice hit." He rolled over to grab his pistol and aimed with both hands.

That fucking despair bug was bulletproof except for the eyes.

Sabine brushed some dust off her shoulder and stalked toward James, a grin on her face like she was having the greatest time of her life. "You know how many souls I've had to take to become powerful enough to face someone like you? Oh, it's been a while since I have faced a worthy enemy. Most men would have died from the punch, let alone hitting the metal."

Shay emptied another clip into the woman, making more holes in her wardrobe but not drawing any blood. If it weren't for a few twitches of Sabine's face, James might have thought she didn't feel the shots.

"You don't get it, do you?" Sabine turned to smile at Shay. "You may have been at the top of your game, but I'm on a different level entirely. I'm much stronger than you might have heard when you were still on the job."

Shay dropped her aim and fired a single round into the necklace. The bullet bounced off in a shower of sparks and for a split second a hint of white and blue peeked from behind the blackness in her eyes.

Nice, Shay. It's my chance.

James rushed toward Sabine, aiming for her right eye. He squeezed off a shot.

"Fuck," he muttered.

Sabine's eyes remained black, with no sign of bruising let alone penetration. She wagged a finger. "I have to say, Mr. Brownstone, I'm a little disappointed. Taking a hit isn't all that impressive when I think about it. I guess in the end you're more legend than truth."

James holstered his pistol and sprinted toward Sabine, slamming into her shoulder-first. The woman let out a soft grunt as she crashed into a pile of two by fours and again her true eyes revealed themselves for a split second.

"Brownstone," Shay called, jogging over to him and reloading her gun. She kept her gaze on Sabine as the woman rose from the pile of wood, snickering.

"I will enjoy adding your souls to my collection," the assassin informed them.

"When I shot the necklace," Shay told him, her voice low. "I saw something in her eyes."

"Same when I hit her," James replied. "Maybe we can wear her down. Concentrate on trying to get the necklace, and I'm going to concen—"

The bounty hunter spun and wrapped Shay in his arms as a two by four slammed into his head and snapped in half.

"Nice reflexes," Sabine called.

James released the wide-eyed Shay and turned to face the assassin again. "You're not gonna kill me with a plank."

"Good," Sabine said. "I wouldn't want this to be disappointing."

Shay nodded to James, and he nodded back. At least they had something approaching a plan.

James rushed toward Sabine, spinning to the side at the last moment to avoid her punch. He slammed his elbow into her head and she staggered back with a grunt. They exchanged a series of quick punches, neither overcoming the defenses of the other.

His arms ached from her blows, and he suspected that without the amulet his bones would have shattered in seconds.

Shay let loose a round directly into the necklace, again summoning sparks and Sabine's true eyes. James followed up with a punch that staggered the woman but didn't send her flying like last time.

Sabine wiped some blood from her cracked lip. "The souls sing inside me, Brownstone. Sing for vengeance."

"Vengeance?" James snarled. "You're the messed-up bitch who killed those people."

"We both deal in death, Brownstone. I just don't let those deaths go to waste."

"Spare me the lecture. I already had someone try mind-fuck crap on this trip and I blew his brains out." James grabbed a nearby two by four and smashed it over the woman's head. Her quick kick in response blasted a jolt of pain through his chest.

Fuck. Did she just break my rib? How the fuck can that even be possible?

Sabine licked her lips. "The souls are stirring in response to your power. Yes. *Yes*." She inhaled deeply. "I don't think I've ever felt such power, but still you can't win." Another bullet struck her necklace. "You think shooting me will work? You're starting to get annoying." She rushed to a row of steel I-beams and grabbed one, spinning and throwing it toward Shay.

Fuck!

The tomb raider ducked to avoid taking four hundred pounds of steel to the face and fired several more rounds. That didn't save her from the follow-up metal spike that nailed her in the left shoulder.

Shay hissed and stumbled backward.

"Shay!" James roared, his heart thundering.

How fucking dare *you, Sabine.*

The tomb raider didn't fall, just let her left arm hang limply and glared at Sabine. "I'm gonna enjoy seeing you die, bitch."

James gritted his teeth and launched himself at Sabine again, ignoring his pain as he launched punch after punch. The vibration of each blow jolted his cracked ribs but he kept up the attack, not wanting to give the assassin any chance to counter.

He managed to land a solid right hook to her face, and followed with a left and then a punch to her stomach. Sabine stumbled back, blood pouring from her nose.

"The way I remember *Beowulf*," James informed her,

"Grendel got his ass kicked and his mommy had to come and deal with the shit. Your mommy gonna come after me when I finish you, Collector?"

James pressed his attack, only to take a kick to his knee. He winced and stumbled back with his knee on fire. Sabine pummeled his body, then grabbed him by the throat and tossed him toward Shay.

The echo of more bullets rang over the construction site as Shay fired round after round into Sabine's necklace.

James took shallow breaths because of the intense pain in his chest and pushed himself up. He wiped the blood from the side of his face and stared at his opponent.

Bruises and cuts marred Sabine's body and face. Despite her smile, she was not unscathed.

Both James and Shay focused their attention on the assassin.

"The last few times you got in good hits or I hit the necklace her eyes stayed normal for longer," Shay murmured.

James responded with a simple grunt. He might be beaten up, but they now had their chance.

"Discussing who will stay and who will run to save themselves?" Sabine called. "I'll let you choose if you want."

James ran toward her, trusting Shay. Her gun blasted behind him, narrowly missing him and striking Sabine. This time he didn't try to punch the assassin but instead tackled her, knocking her into a nearby pile of girders. He grabbed her head and slammed it repeatedly into a steel girder.

The assassin let out a low growl and kicked the bounty hunter off her, hopping to her feet and wiping some blood out of her eyes and off her mouth. Another bullet struck her necklace.

"You two are stubborn," Sabine remarked. Blood stains now covered her pale face like some sort of twisted mask. "And I apologize for my earlier insult, Mr. Brownstone. You do live up to your reputation."

James charged again, but the woman sidestepped, striking his neck with her elbow and kneeing him in the stomach. She followed up with two punches that sent him into the treads of a bulldozer and leapt on the stunned man, ignoring several more shots from Shay and slamming fist after fist into his face.

Stars filled his vision as his head snapped back again and again to meet the metal of the bulldozer. Blood and pain blinded him.

"Brownstone!" Shay yelled. "They're white for a second each time now."

James grunted and threw up an arm to block Sabine's punch. He launched his other fist into her head, knocking the small woman off him even though the blow to her face felt like punching steel.

"Give me a countdown, Shay," the bounty hunter yelled. He grabbed a metal spike from the ground, ignoring the throbbing in his chest and head.

Sabine took several deep breaths. "You die, Brownstone."

"Three…" Shay began.

James raised the spike and stepped forward.

"Two…"

The assassin raised her fists.

"One…"

James charged and Shay's gun spat a bullet out, which struck the pendant. Sabine's eyes turned white and the bounty hunter slammed the spike into the woman's head.

Sabine's eyes widened as the metal pierced her skull and she stumbled backward, blinking. "Not...possible."

"It helps to have friends," James told her, holding his ribs. "But you're a bitch, so you don't have any."

The assassin collapsed, her astonished expression frozen on her face as she stopped breathing. Her obsidian necklace exploded in a shower of orange-blue sparks.

James hissed and fell to his knees. He could only hope that the souls the woman had collected were now free.

Shay limped over to him, holding her wounded shoulder. She took a deep breath, pulled out the spike, and downed her healing potion seconds later.

"Fuck," the tomb raider muttered. "That wasn't fun."

"Can you drive back to the hotel?" James asked, forcing himself to his feet despite the pain. "I left my healing potions there."

"Are you shitting me now?"

"Nope. Didn't think she'd be so tough."

Shay scrubbed a hand over her face as the wound on her shoulder started knitting itself closed. "She could have killed you, even with the amulet. Maybe...you know, you should have thought about the wish."

James shook his head. "Not my wish. I'd rather live without stealing it and give it to Alison. For now, let's get back to the hotel so I can take the potion."

"You can use one of mine."

"No, they... Normal potions don't work on me."

Shay's eyes narrowed. "I see." She nodded as if she'd

figured something out. "Bring your fucking potion when we raid the Harriken, idiot."

James snorted. "Sure thing, Mom." He nodded toward the dead Sabine. "I guess I should clean up the body with the Professor's toy."

"Yeah, and make it quick. I'm surprised the cops aren't already here."

James stared at Sabine for a few seconds. "Some assassin, huh?"

Shay shook her head. "She wasn't an assassin. She was a killer."

22

The next afternoon James patted himself down, checking his loadout. His pistols, knives, grenades, and potions were all present. He didn't want to repeat his mistake with Sabine, and could only assume there would be a few artifact-wielding enforcers in the Harriken headquarters.

Shay checked her weapon's magazine. "Not that I think it's a problem, but just to check—you sure about ignoring the third bounty?"

"Yeah. He's not as bad as the despair bug or the serial killer. He's a piece of shit, but I'm about to lay out a lot of those. I just want to get this over with and get back to America. I want some Jessie Rae's."

A light knock came from the door and their hands went to their pistols. James nodded at Shay as she moved closer to the door and she edged up on it, not standing directly in front until she was right next to it.

She leaned over to peek through the peephole. "Looks like a cop," she mouthed.

Yeah, I figured they might show up eventually.

James holstered his weapon and slipped on his gray coat. "Let him in."

The tomb raider frowned, holstered her own weapon, and opened the door.

A handsome middle-aged Japanese man in a dark suit entered. A few stripes of white ran through his dark hair.

He stepped inside and gave them a shallow bow. "Mr. Brownstone, do you have a moment?" His gaze cut to Shay with a faint question.

James shrugged. "Who are you?"

"Detective Sakamoto," the man replied. "I was asked to come by and speak with you about your plans. Let me first say that on behalf of the Japanese people, I would like to thank you for your defeat of the despair bug and handling the issue with the serial killer. We're very impressed with your efficiency."

"Thanks."

Guessing a big 'but' is coming.

Detective Sakamoto gave a thin smile. "But please note there is no organizational bounty on the Harriken."

Yeah.

"Yeah, a cop told me that when I arrived."

Shay and James exchanged glances.

The detective shrugged. "However, I've also been informed there are some emergency gas line repairs that have to be performed in parts of Azabu. Very important repairs required immediately."

"Really? That's, uh, interesting." James resisted laughing. Azabu was where the Harriken headquarters were located.

"Because of this," the detective continued, "as of this morning, police are redirecting traffic from that area, and will for the entirety of this week. We're concerned about...gas explosions harming civilians, though it'd be...useful if the work were finished earlier so we could send the police elsewhere."

So that's how they want to play it—plausible deniability? Let the violent foreigner take out the thugs. Shit. Overly complicated, but it works for me. I'm not in it for the money this time.

James exchanged glances with Shay and she shrugged.

The bounty hunter cleared his throat. "What if someone was to go to Azabu and, you know, speed up the process of fixing the gas leak. What would you say to that?"

The detective nodded. "I think anyone who could do that would find that quiet appreciation sometimes works better than public praise. Now, the local police have to concentrate on keeping civilians away from any potential explosions and they aren't going to interfere with a public works specialist in the performance of his duty."

James grinned. "That's me. I'm a great public works specialist, and I was thinking I should go check on that gas leak right away."

Detective Sakamoto bowed. "We would appreciate that, and I'll also note that it will be easier for people evaluating the damage after the fact if certain people weren't around to draw attention to themselves." Without another word, the detective stepped out of the hotel room and closed the door.

Shay whistled. "So no help, but no interference. Wonder what changed their minds?"

"Probably me taking out that serial killer without blowing up half of Kabukichō. Or maybe they figure if this all goes south it'll be easy to pin the blame on the crazy foreigner. Don't give a shit, really. It means we have the go-ahead to take out those Harriken bastards and no one will get caught in the crossfire."

"It also means the Harriken know we're coming. I mean, they aren't idiots. If the cops are keeping people away from their building, they have to know you're coming."

"Yeah, but they don't know when. Might as well hit them before they get too entrenched."

"I agree." Shay stared at his chest. "Are you wearing it?"

James shook his head. "I...don't need it. I think I'll be okay."

"Are you fucking kidding me? You used it last time you took on the Harriken. This isn't the time to be stubborn, Brownstone."

"I'm sure I could have done fine without it."

James shrugged. Even *he* didn't really believe what he was saying. If he'd not had the amulet during the last Harriken raid he probably wouldn't have made it halfway up the building.

Shay frowned. "If you hadn't worn that thing when you took on Sabine you'd be dead now. I don't get it. It freaks you out just because it whispers or whatever? Get over it and stop being such a bitch."

James grunted. "It changes me. Gives me powers.

232

Sabine's necklace collected souls. How the fuck do I know *I'm* not doing that? For all I know, it's demonic."

"Is that what that priest at your church is putting in your head?"

James narrowed his eyes, thinking for a moment she was talking about Father Thomas. Then realized she must be talking about Father McCartney.

"It's just something I've been thinking about," James mumbled.

Shay heaved a great sigh. "I wanted to wait a little longer while I researched things, but I think it's time I told you my theory. It's got nothing to do with demons."

Trey rubbed his hands together as he sat in the driver's seat of his F-350, which was parked down the street from Brownstone's apartment. He loved the truck. He accepted he'd never be a badass motherfucker like James Brownstone, but at least he had the same truck now. That had to mean something.

Got to think like motherfucking Brownstone. He ain't scared of no 5-0. They are his bitches. I need to make them my *bitches.*

The gang leader spared a glance at Sergeant Mack, who sat in the passenger seat with a shotgun in his lap.

Two dark vans cruised down the street and Trey whistled.

"See, I *knew* them bitches would be showing up. Told you my boys heard the right shit."

"Thanks for letting me know, Trey."

Trey snorted. "Shit, motherfucker. This ain't for you,

Mr. Po Po. It's for Mr. Brownstone. That motherfucker knows about respect being a two-way street."

The vans screeched to a halt and the doors flew open. Several Demon Generals hopped out of the vans.

"When that bitch-ass gets back from Japan," shouted one of the gang members. "I want him to wet his pants about how he ain't got no shit."

Sergeant Mack lifted a walkie-talkie to his mouth. "All units go. All units go." He threw open the door and hopped out, shotgun at the ready. "LAPD! On the ground!"

The Demon Generals' hands dropped toward the guns stuck in their waistbands. Sirens blared and red and blue lights flashed as several cop cars screamed down the street and uniformed officers popped up from behind two unmarked SUVs on the other side of the street.

The gang members dropped to their knees and laced their fingers together behind their heads as the cops swarmed them.

Trey laughed and reached into a brown paper bag to pull out his Nana's specialty: a jelly and butter sandwich. Normal butter, not peanut butter, which was for bitch-ass motherfuckers.

"There goes some of my competition. Who knew doing a good thing could help my motherfucking ass so much?"

James stared at Shay. "Your theory?"

The tomb raider averted her eyes and took a deep breath. "You're not from Earth, Brownstone. That's what I think."

"Nah."

Shay's gaze snapped back his way. "Nah?"

"They checked that shit. I don't know all the details, but they had some sort of way of doing a magical test to check if I was from Oriceran or traveled there."

"Yeah, I know you're not from Oriceran."

Now it was James' turn to be surprised. "You *know*?"

Shay stepped forward until she was so close her hot breath fanned across his face. She grabbed his cheeks with her hands and tilted his head down until he was looking straight at her. She let her hands drop to his shoulders.

James' heart rate increased.

What the fuck is she doing?

Shay sighed. "Before I tell you this you've got to know something. No matter if what I say is true I still give a shit about you, okay?"

James' stomach tightened. Nobody started an explanation that way who didn't end with some reveal like a person was the direct descendant of Cain or some other shit.

The bounty hunter swallowed. "Shay, you don't give a shit about any man."

Shay chuckled. "Well, I didn't, and maybe I still don't. But this is different, because you're not just *any* man."

"What the fuck does that mean?"

"You're from another world." Shay lifted a hand. "And I don't mean Oriceran."

"Okay, now what the fuck does that mean?" James shook his head, totally lost.

"It's simple, Brownstone. You're from a different planet.

Not Oriceran. Like alien, from the stars. Little-green-men-in-spaceships kind of aliens."

James stumbled back until he hit the door, then ran a hand over his face.

Strange birthmarks. Ridges. He'd just assumed they were minor deformities. They made him ugly, but they hadn't slowed him down.

"You really think so?" James asked quietly.

"Yeah, I do. Look, after everything you told me, I'm guessing you were sent here somehow by your parents to keep you safe."

"And the amulet? You think that was to keep me safe?"

"I don't know. Some of the glyphs I've been able to decipher don't really make it seem like it's a protection thing...not much." Shay blew out a breath. "It's a weapon, really. That's my theory." She frowned. "No, that's not right. It's not so much a weapon as a tool for turning someone *into* a weapon, I think. A few of those glyphs have something to do with war."

James ran his hand over his shirt until he felt the lump of the amulet. "I'm some sort of living weapon?"

"I guess. Maybe." Shay shrugged. "I can't be sure. So, yeah, it's a good thing to maybe not use it 24/7."

"But you want me to use it against the Harriken?"

"This isn't a bounty, Brownstone. This is a war. Use it this time, then dial it back until we understand it."

James pulled out the amulet with its metal separator still attached and stared at it. "I've thought a lot about why I became a bounty hunter. I wondered if I did it to get revenge for Father Thomas, or because I watched too much *Lone Ranger* as a kid. If what you're saying is true...

fuck, I'm just becoming what I was supposed to be." He gritted his teeth. "I don't know if I like the idea that I'm some sort of weapon."

"A weapon's not evil or good, Brownstone. It's all about who's holding it. Come on, you have to know that by now. You could have been one evil son of a bitch, but you're not." Shay snorted. "I was an evil son of a bitch, and I don't even have your abilities."

"If I'm the weapon, who is holding me?"

Shay shrugged. "For now, I guess maybe me?"

James chuckled. "Don't know how I feel about that."

"Put your big-boy pants on and let's go kill some Harriken. You'll feel better after that."

23

Grandfather sighed when a Harriken subordinate ran into the room. The Harriken leader looked up from the small table he was kneeling in front of and waited for the man to speak.

His subordinate bowed deep. "Grandfather, most of the reinforcements from Osaka, Nagoya, Yokohama, and Kyoto have arrived. A large group from Sapporo have arrived as well, but others have been held up."

"Excellent. I'm unconcerned about the stragglers. They won't be able to share in the stories of our glory, but I'm sure that we have more than sufficient men to battle Brownstone now. "

Grandfather stroked his chin. The bulk of the might of the Harriken were now concentrated in the Tokyo head-quarters. Many would undoubtedly die during Brown-stone's attack, but there was no way the foreign bounty hunter could defeat the strongest and brightest of the

Harriken in the heart of their empire in the greatest city in the world.

No, the legend of James Brownstone would end at the hands of the Harriken. He would be the example that even the strongest and greatest of men was nothing before their powerful organization.

It was fortunate that the Harriken spies in the police department tipped the group off that the police were going to isolate their area. When Grandfather had received that news he'd immediately put out the order for reinforcements. If they'd waited until they saw the police deploy it might have been too late. Recognizing that his men would defeat Brownstone wasn't the same thing as believing it wouldn't be difficult.

A drone spotted Brownstone driving in their general direction, but he'd jammed the machine, and now they couldn't be sure when he would attack—only that it was soon. Not only that, but he had a companion. A woman. They could only assume she was an associate with at least some similar level of lethality.

Unfortunately, they hadn't gotten a good image of her face from the drone's camera so they couldn't identify her.

Twice the danger for twice the glory.

The man's heart raced with an excitement he hadn't felt in decades. The Harriken had grown too far and too fast because their enemies were unworthy and weak.

Brownstone had to be destroyed to reclaim their honor, but the man had provided a valuable service. He'd reminded the Harriken that victory was always fleeting.

"And the authorities?" Grandfather inquired. "What are they doing now?"

Brownstone was only one man, and his whore was only one woman. Two people, even powerful people, would be manageable. Hundreds of police storming the building would be far more difficult to handle.

"They're doing nothing."

"Nothing?"

His subordinate frowned. "Nothing besides keeping people out of the area. We haven't seen any anti-magic teams. No special assault teams, and only a few drones. They've brought in a lot of patrol officers, but they've let our men through with no resistance. They are also staying a huge distance from the building. They actually moved their men farther back than when they set up."

Grandfather narrowed his eyes. "Cowards. They don't even intend to fight." He sneered. "They will let this foreigner fight for them." He laughed. "No matter. It makes this far less difficult. Once Brownstone is dead, perhaps the police will know our wrath. I thought they respected our right to rule the underworld, but the first chance they get they try to kill us. Their hopes are misplaced in this man and his whore."

"Are they?" The man looked away. "Maybe we should consider other options."

"*Other options*? You suggest we flee from our headquarters? From this, the heart of the Harriken empire?"

The Harriken underling swallowed. "Brownstone has killed so many. Are we sure we can win? The men in America weren't weak."

"No, but they weren't led by me." Grandfather looked down at the enchanted *Masamune tachi* lying across his table. "Brownstone is powerful. No one denies that, and I will grant him the respect he's earned as a worthy foe, but he's just a man. He has trinkets, but so do we. He bleeds, and his heart can stop." He nodded at the sword. "I trust that our bravest men have been given our best weapons?"

"Yes, Grandfather. We've taken everything out of the vault. Special teams have been set up on each floor."

"Damage to the building is irrelevant. We can always repair it. Does everyone understand that?"

"Yes, Grandfather."

The Harriken leader ran his finger along the magical blade. "All this is as it should be. Destiny has guided us to this moment. We should have never relied on pathetic hitmen or assassins. We should have sent an invitation to Brownstone and challenged him directly. No matter. Once he dies today no one will ever question the Harriken again, and our power will stretch to every city on this planet." He curled his hand into a fist. "Come, Brownstone. Come to your death."

"This was easier than I thought it would be," Shay told James as they stepped out of a maintenance tunnel into the underground parking lot beneath the Harriken headquarters. "Their electronic security is pretty pathetic."

James lowered the two heavy duffel bags he'd been carrying over his shoulders to the ground and adjusted his backpack. "Because they think they are too badass for anyone to mess with them."

"Yeah, but they also know we're coming."

James tossed Shay one of the duffle bags. "They also expect me to kick open the front door."

"That is more your style. Well, we still have to execute the next part of your plan." Shay opened the duffel bag.

"This time I'll try to be more thorough." James shrugged. "I don't want to have to travel again to deal with Harriken fuckers." He started pulling plastic explosive charges from his duffel bag. "I'm no demolitions expert. Just set 'em up at all the supports, I guess."

"We brought enough to blow up half of Tokyo. Did you make sure the cops pulled their perimeter back?"

"Yeah."

Shay nodded and pulled out explosives from her bag as well, then jogged over to a concrete pillar and pulled off an adhesive strip to place the charge on it. "Man, look at all these sweet cars."

James glanced around the parking garage. A good eighty percent were shiny sports cars, with a few creepy vans for good measure. Couldn't be a proper criminal gang without a few creepy vans for when you needed to grab someone, put a bag over their head, and toss them inside. He spotted only a handful of trucks.

Don't these fuckers ever have to haul anything?

He placed a few more charges. "Need more trucks, especially Fords."

Shay laughed. "Yeah, I'm sure a bunch of Japanese gangsters are going to ride around Tokyo in American-made trucks. That makes perfect sense."

James shrugged. "Quality is quality. Ford makes good trucks."

"Yeah, I'll stick to my Fiat."

The pair spent the next five minutes planting the rest of their charges.

With the first step of the plan finished, James pulled a small triangular amulet that appeared to be made of frosted quartz from his bag and slipped it around his neck.

Shay peered at him. "Another amulet? Double bling? What, are you a rapper now, Brownstone?"

James grunted. "Yeah, Sir Kicks-Ass-A-Lot." He pulled out an identical amulet and tossed it to Shay.

The tomb raider snatched it out of the air and eyed it with suspicion. "Another loan from the Professor?"

"Yeah."

"That man must be expecting a hell of a dirty-limerick show."

James grimaced. "Don't remind me." He gestured at the necklace. "Put it on, and don't lose it if you don't want to die."

"That's reassuring. I don't recognize it. What does it do?"

"You'll see soon enough." James then fished out a little clay urn with cuneiform symbols near the top and set it on top of some asshole's bright-yellow GTO.

Fucking gaudy. It's a good thing I'm blowing it up.

The bounty hunter grunted as he remembered the Professor's words about the urn.

And I've brought you another present, lad. This one you don't even have to bring back. Some things are useful, but we shouldn't like using them. Kind of like nuclear weapons that way.

"Okay," Shay said, "and what does that Sumerian urn do?"

"You'll also see that soon enough. Basic version is, it kicks a lot of ass."

Shay laughed. "Of course."

Fifteen minutes later James and Shay were back outside removing the last of their supplies from the trunk of the rental car. They dropped their backpacks into it after retrieving all the goodies.

"Hope this car doesn't get blown up," the bounty hunter mumbled as he closed the trunk. "I'd like to go a while without having to replace a rental car."

Eventually, no one's gonna rent me a car.

"It's like I told you before. I couldn't spot any snipers with the drone. I think these assholes believe they can take us as long as they get us inside." Shay pointed toward the glass doors in the distance. "You can even see a few of the fuckers watching us, so if they wanted to start dropping bullets on high toward us they could."

James looked that way. Shay was right. The Harriken might not have caught them in the parking garage, but they knew they were there. Now it was time to give them the show they expected of him.

He picked up a rocket launcher he'd hidden on the opposite side of the car and the men near the doors scattered as James hoisted it to his shoulder.

James glanced at Shay. "Okay, I think I have their attention. You ready?"

The tomb raider nodded grimly. "Yeah, I'll head to the

side door. Give me about a minute to get into position after the first shot."

James nodded. "Just so you Harriken assholes know," the bounty hunter muttered to himself, "this is very, *very* fucking personal." He launched the rocket.

24

The rocket flew toward the entrance, exploding on impact and sending a plume of fire, smoke, and glass fragments into the air.

James waited about a minute, then grabbed the second rocket from the ground, loaded the launcher, and aimed again.

"This shit's fun. I should do this more often."

The second rocket zoomed through the demolished entryway deep enough that only the loud boom and the smoke spilling out proved it hit anything. A few distant screams sounded.

Sorry, douchebags.

James yanked out his .45 and jogged toward the smoke-spewing maw that had once been the entrance to the Harriken's headquarters. His arrival at the ruins of the entrance confirmed the destruction. Glass, wood, and metal were strewn about the entrance along with several charred bodies.

"Seems like I keep fucking up your doors."

Movement on his left had him spinning with his gun raised. The source was Shay, her gun in her hands.

"Killed three guys on the way here," the woman told him with a grin. "Things aren't starting out well for the home team."

"Okay, let's go."

They charged down the hallway and a half-dozen Harriken spun around the corners, sub-machine guns ready. Shay and James put them down without even slowing their pace.

The amulet whispered in the back of James' mind, but it wasn't as insistent today. Maybe it didn't care because it was getting exactly what it wanted: lots of sacrifices.

You like that, you angry alien piece of shit? Or have you been telling me to stop this whole time and finally just gave the fuck up?

The heavy footsteps of reinforcements keyed James into the need to ready a frag grenade, so he pulled the pin and tossed it. The new arrivals didn't even have time to realize what was happening before they died in a shower of flame and shrapnel.

"Yeah, take that, fuckers!"

The roar of a rocket sounded from behind him. James spun to see a bloodied man holding a rocket launcher. A triumphant smile appeared on his face just before he collapsed, screaming, "Die, *oni!*"

"Fuck," James yelled.

Shay leapt into a nearby hallway as the bounty hunter threw himself to the ground. The rocket exploded into the wall and the force slammed James into the other wall. The amulet's whispers became more insistent.

Oh, it's not okay when I got blown up. Thanks for the newsflash.

"Brownstone?" Shay shouted. "You still alive?"

James pushed himself off the ground, wiping some blood from a minor cut. A few minor burns and lacerations were a small price to pay for being caught in a rocket explosion. The amulet might be whispering more, but it was still keeping his ass alive.

"Talk about ironic reversal!" Shay laughed.

"I'm glad you found that funny."

"You've got to admit it was a *little* funny."

The bounty hunter shrugged. "I killed people when I used mine." He took point and rushed off without another word.

They jogged farther down the hall and the door to the main stairs came into sight. Several Harriken popped out of side rooms and got off rounds, but when their bullets struck the amulet-enhanced James he just grunted. Shay and James' counterattack left the hallway littered with bodies and the walls splattered with blood.

James and Shay halted at the door and reloaded.

"Shay, let me go first in case they have some sort of fireball or rocket launcher or weredragon or some shit," the bounty hunter rumbled.

The tomb raider nodded. "Give me a countdown."

"One... two...three." James' jump-kick sent the metal door flying inward and it crashed into a concrete wall with a dull thud that echoed throughout the stairwell.

James rushed into the stairwell, his gun aimed upward. A shower of bullets rained from men on the second-floor landing and he emptied his .45 into them until the eight enforcers lay dead on the ground or splayed out on the stairs. The assault left a few new cuts on him, but nothing serious.

You need to bring out the big guns if you want to have a fucking chance, assholes.

Shay followed James in once his quick kills ended the lead storm. "Shit. This is gonna take a while if we're going floor by floor. We got ten floors of this crap. I wish these fuckers would stand and fight in a big group."

"Pest control is always obnoxious. Always have to look under that one dark crevice for the last roach."

Shay snickered.

When they rushed to the second floor no one else shot at them. James stopped before opening the door, hard way or otherwise.

"We go in guns blazing?" Shay asked. She tapped a silver bracelet on her wrist. "That should take care of the cameras on this floor."

James shook his head. "Nope. We got lucky on the first floor. They'll probably be artifact bastards soon. If we don't play it smart it'll slow things down."

Shay scoffed. "We've got your amulet. I think we've got the advantage."

Even though that was true, James was still worried about the risk. Shay was tough and good with a weapon, but she couldn't take a point-blank shot from a gun like he could. That meant he needed to make sure he was taking the brunt of any high-powered assaults, and that he needed to use all the tools available to him.

"It's time to show you what that urn was about." James glanced at Shay to confirm she was wearing the quartz necklace. "Whatever you do, keep that necklace on." He reached underneath his previously merely shabby but now hole-filled gray coat and pulled out a small golden rod about six inches in length. Swirls of platinum ran up the length.

"Is this another 'You'll see' thing?"

James grunted, lifted the rod, and snapped it with both hands. "Yeah, you'll see real fucking soon."

Shay's eyes widened, and the bounty hunter could almost see the calculations in her head.

"What the fuck, Brownstone? You breaking the Professor's shit?"

"Nah, he said this and the urn were kind of a one-use deal."

Chilling screams sounded from the first floor.

James shrugged. "Guess we missed some."

Shay glanced at the opening to the first floor, uncertainty on her face. "What did that thing do?"

Is this evil? Fuck if I know.

More screams sounded, and James remained in place. He needed what the artifact had summoned before he busted down any more doors.

A skeletal ghost-warrior faded through the wall and entered the stairwell, followed by another, and then more. Soon seven of the specters marched together.

Shay raised her gun, her eyes wide. "What the fuck are those?"

"The Professor didn't give me the history, just told me to set the urn at the lowest point and break the rod when

I'm ready. Those things will kill people using magic. Guess we missed a few artifact users on the first floor. Once they get to the highest point they'll destroy the only remaining sources of magic: themselves."

"Brownstone, I hate to break this to you, but those things are coming right toward us. We both have potions on us, and I'm not sure if your alien amulet there counts as magic or not."

"The other amulet I'm wearing and the one I gave you will shield us from them."

The skeletal warriors marched up the stairs in eerie silence.

James stared at the conjured beings and his stomach tightened. The Professor had promised him that the seven warriors weren't true skeletons and that he wasn't practicing necromancy or toying with souls, but the death-dealing ghost skeletons walking up the stairs didn't leave his mind at ease.

Spooked, he shook the thoughts out of his head and kicked in the door without warning Shay. A loud buzz preceded a bolt of red energy blasting into his chest and sending him sailing backward, and a burning sensation covered the spot where it had hit. He slammed against the stairwell wall and fell to the floor.

"Brownstone!" Shay yelled.

James pushed himself off the ground, wincing at the burn. "I'm still alive, but, yeah, that hurt a little."

I think that shit would have blasted right through me without the amulet.

The skeletons walked past James into the room, some through the doorway, some through the wall. Gunfire and more red blasts flashed and screams echoed down the hallway

James rushed back up the stairs past a concerned Shay.

"Don't you fucking scare me like that again, dickwad," she hissed.

When they entered the room they found two men lying on the ground with their throats ripped out, their blood staining the benches filling the room. Two dozen more were firing at the skeletons. Their bullets weren't passing through the apparitions, but they also didn't seem to be doing much damage.

The skeletons were ignoring the attackers and forming a circle around the two dead men, one of whom had a wand lying next to him.

James and Shay took advantage of the Harriken's confusion to start putting bullets into their heads, but after the first few casualties the rest returned fire. But the surprise was too lopsided, and soon all the men lay dead or dying on the floor.

One of the skeletons reached down to pick up the oaken-shafted, ruby-tipped wand. It stuck the wand into its mouth and gobbled it down an inch at a time.

"Huh. Did not expect that."

"That's not something you see every day," Shay remarked.

"Let's go," the bounty hunter muttered. "We've got a whole building full of people to kill."

After an orgy of bloodletting as they proceeded from floor

to floor, the bounty hunter and the tomb raider stood on the tenth floor in front of carved double doors leading to what James assumed were the private chambers of the leader of the Harriken. Dead bodies lay all around them and little of the floor or walls remained free of blood.

James had lost count of how many Harriken had died after two hundred. The amulet's whispers weren't loud, but they'd been steady and pervasive for most of the running battle.

Burns and cuts covered James' body, along with a deep gash from some sort of enchanted clockwork attack cat. Shay had been grazed by a few bullets on the previous floor.

The skeletons, still silent as ever, turned on each other, clawing, biting, and ripping. They spilled no blood, but each blow took a piece until only a pile of slowly fading ghostly bones remained.

Shay stared down at the remains of the skeletons and gestured toward the door. "Guess the Head Asshole must have some sort of shielding artifact or something, or the Bone Squad would have gone after him." She nodded. "Or maybe a nullification spell or something around the office to protect him from spying. Guess we'll have to finish him ourselves."

"Good. I fucking need to end this myself rather than relying on shit like that." James gritted his teeth. "I hated to use those things," he grumped, "but otherwise there was no fucking way we would have survived with all the magic shit the Harriken were pulling out of their asses."

Shay winced as she leaned against the wall. "Hey, I'm not complaining."

"I fucking *hate* using magic." James tapped his chest where the amulet was fused with him. "I don't know if this is magic or weird alien tech shit or whatever, but I hate this too."

"Sometimes you have to fight magic with magic." Shay shrugged. "That's the world we live in now."

"Yeah, but it isn't simple."

"*Life* isn't simple, Brownstone. Get over it."

James grunted, then pulled out a healing potion and downed the contents. Shay followed his lead.

"I guess it's time for Badass Maximus," he rumbled. "I wonder what kind of bullshit he's got in store."

Shay sighed.

"What's wrong?"

"The bigger they are, the more they bore you to tears with speeches." Shay gestured to the door. "It's your big enemy, not mine, so you do the honors."

James smiled, feeling a little better thanks to the healing potion and the demise—or at least departure—of the strange ghost warriors. "You're right." He kicked open the door and stepped inside.

The leader of the Harriken stood behind a small table that was low to the ground. He was clad in an elaborately patterned kimono and held a *tachi*.

"I am Grandfather. I lead the Harriken, and I will be the man to take your life, James Brownstone."

James didn't think the guy looked that old, all things considered, but he wasn't about to waste time bickering over ceremonial titles with some asshole he was about to kill.

The bounty hunter grunted. "That a *Masamune?*"

"Of course, Brownstone," Grandfather replied with a smirk. "I applaud you for making it this far, but we both know you will fall before this sword."

"Maybe." James shrugged. "It didn't have to be this way. You fuckers had plenty of chances to leave me alone."

"The Harriken do not cower before anyone, let alone a single man."

James snorted. "I carved through all of your men like they were bitches who had never held a gun or a sword before."

Grandfather sneered. "Such arrogance. You think you are powerful because you killed some men today? You're *nothing.* I took the Harriken from a mere shadow to one of the most powerful groups in the global underworld." He pointed with the sword. "And I'm not some Oriceran *oni.*"

"Because I'm tough you're calling me a bitch? That's bullshit. I'm not the pussy who hid behind an army of thugs."

"You're nothing but a mistake. You should have stayed on your own world, you Oriceran freak."

James grunted. "I'm not fucking Oriceran, and none of this changes how all your bad boys got their asses kicked by me in the end."

"I killed my first man when I was twelve, Brownstone. Do you know why?"

"He was fucking your mom after your dad left?"

Grandfather narrowed his eyes. "Because he disrespected me. All who have disrespected me have died, just as you will. I've killed so many over the years that I don't even remember most of them."

"I've killed so many guys today that I can't remember the faces of the guys I took out on the first floor."

The older man raised his sword. "Come at me, then. Show me the might of Brownstone before I cut you down."

A gunshot rang out. Grandfather's eyes widened as blood poured from a new hole in his head and slumped over the table. The *tachi* fell, embedding itself in the wood.

Several seconds passed before James registered that the man was dead. He looked at Shay, who holstered her 9mm.

The tomb raider shrugged. "It was either that or get a ruler out and offer to measure your dicks." She snorted. "Fuck, Brownstone, were you going to *talk* him to death?"

James stared down at the dead Harriken leader, surprised that he didn't feel that different despite everything being over. He shrugged.

Well, I guess there aren't many Harriken left to come after me now.

Shay hurried over to a computer on a small desk in the corner and plugged a thumb drive into a USB port, then grabbed her phone.

"Who you calling?"

"Peyton. I figured he could mess around and copy shit before you blow up the place." Shay adjusted her phone in her hand. "Yeah, it's me. I'm in. Get what you can as quickly as you can. This building's not gonna exist much longer. Yeah. Okay. Right." She hung up the phone. "Let's grab some shit and get out of here."

"Everyone shut the fuck up!" Tyler yelled.

Everyone in the Black Sun complied and turned their hostile glares on the bartender.

Maria took a sip of her beer and wondered what the slimeball was up to now.

"I've just been made aware of an impending important announcement." Tyler pulled out his phone and tapped in a few commands. The TV on the wall turned black.

"What the fuck, Tyler?" yelled a man.

A scraping sound came from the TV and the black gave way to the image of a ten-story building that had obviously suffered some damage.

Maria narrowed her eyes. She recognized the building from her background briefings—it was the Harriken's headquarters in the Azabu neighborhood of Tokyo.

"What you see here is the Harriken headquarters," came Brownstone's familiar grinding voice from the TV.

"Son of a bitch," Maria muttered. She was having trouble sorting through her feelings. She'd bet that he would survive, but, on some level she'd hoped he wouldn't.

A loud roar came from the TV and the image shook for several seconds. Parts of the tall building fell, which triggered a cascade of floors collapsing until the building had imploded, leaving only a pile of rubble and a huge cloud of dust.

"Well, it *was* the Harriken headquarters. Somebody seems to have blown it up."

A chorus of "damn!" rose from everyone in the bar; everyone except Maria.

Wish you would have pulled that stunt here. Then I could have cuffed you and stuffed you. I'm not even gonna bother to call the Japanese police and tell them to get a voice-print match.

You probably have them sucking your cock already. But this shit isn't over, Brownstone. Once you're back in America, your ass will be mine eventually.

The next day, Maria sat in her office looking through an email response to a request for information on a suspect, in this case the unidentified female they'd tagged in the drone feed from LAX.

They had nothing on the woman. Absolutely fucking nothing.

Maria found that hard to believe. Even people who never left their apartments had some sort of profile, but this woman was like a ghost—and that smelled too clean. Even with the glasses, the algorithms should have been able to turn up some matches.

"Somebody's been scrubbing her presence. Doesn't matter. Something will come up eventually, chickadee, and if you are running with Brownstone you *can't* be clean."

Maria clicked a few times to move the file to her "To-do" folder.

"I'll get back to this shit when I have time."

25

James took a deep breath and slowly let it out before sliding open the confessional door and stepping inside.

"Bless me, Father, for I have sinned."

"How many, James?" Father McCartney asked, his voice weary. "I'm assuming this is about that incident in Tokyo?"

The bounty hunter winced. If his confessor was starting off with his first name, he'd gone straight from annoyed to deeply concerned about the state of the bounty hunter's soul.

"Yeah. How many? Don't know. Every last one who was there. I decided to go old-school to send the message. Burned their building to the ground and poured salt on the top so nothing will grow for generations."

"Did you have any other choice?"

James sighed. "I don't know. I tried to send them a message the first time, but that didn't stop them. Instead, they sent all those hitmen after me. So I tried to send them a message a second time here."

"And what happened? I didn't see anything on the news after the earlier incident in town."

"They hired assassins, Father. Top-grade. One came here, and I decided to take the fight to the other four. I can't leave this sh...stuff alone anymore. Not with Alison. I can't take a risk that someone might hurt her."

The priest let out a weary sigh. "The deeper into violence you go, the more this sort of thing will happen. You have to know that."

James let out a laugh. "Guess you won't accept 'They started it' any better now that I'm a man than you did when I was a kid?"

Father McCartney chuckled. "I fear for your soul, but I don't weep for wicked men who have been made to pay for their life of preying upon others. What we sow, we reap."

Should you even be praying for me? If Shay's right, I'm not even human. Did our Savior sacrifice himself for humans or for everyone?

James took a deep breath and let it out. "I'm pretty sure it's over this time, at least."

"I hope so, James, for your sake. Spend some time in prayer for the next few days, reflecting on what our Lord wants from us all. Take a week away from your job and try to remember the humanity you're protecting rather than being crushed by the darkness of the evil you're used to dealing with."

"I will, Father. Thank you, Father."

"Go with God, child."

James slid open the door.

"James," Father McCartney called, causing the bounty hunter to stop. "Again, I wanted to thank you for the stock. I can't express how much good it has done for both the church and the orphanage. Whatever you feel about what just happened, remember the good you've done that doesn't involve violence."

James smiled. "Just making sure there are plenty of future barbeque lovers in the world, Father."

James pushed into the Leanan Sídhe, his palms sweaty and his heart pumping. He glanced around the crowd, looking for people gathered around individuals.

No one's singing or saying shit. Good, didn't step into some Bard of Filth night.

The bounty hunter let out a sigh of relief as he made his way to the Professor's favorite booth in the back. Shay sat across from the older man.

James slipped into the booth next to her and set a brief-case in front of the Professor. "That's all your shit back, except for that urn and rod, but you said those were no big deal."

The Professor nodded and took a sip from the mug in front of him. "Aye, lad. I kept those things around because I thought they eventually might be helpful in a situation like the one you were just in." A huge grin appeared on his face. "But I hope you're practicing your dirty limericks."

James groaned. "You're serious about that shit?"

"More serious than I am about beer." The Professor

gulped some of the amber liquid. "And beer is the most important thing God ever inspired in man."

Shay snickered. "Make sure you send me a text when Brownstone's gonna perform. I have a feeling this chicken-shit won't tell me."

"Of course, Miz Carson. I wouldn't allow you to miss such an epic performance."

Everyone's fucking conspiring against me. I better leave before they get some ideas.

James stood. "I think I better get going."

The Professor laughed. "There's no competition tonight, lad. You don't have to run off."

"Just being careful. I'll pay my debt, but I have a few things to clean up first."

The Professor chuckled. "Before you leave…" He nodded to James and Shay in turn. "I was wondering if you might be interested in a job soon. This time it's in Egypt."

Shay shrugged. "It pays in money, right? I'm not interested in dirty limericks."

"Yes, money, but I'll throw in the dirty limericks." The Professor glanced between the two. "We can discuss this another night. You both need some time to rest between all of your traveling and interesting tourist activities."

James nodded and headed for the door. He was almost there when he felt someone grab his hand. He turned and saw that it was a smiling Shay.

Someone who can understand me. Someone who'll accept me for who I am, even if I am a fucking alien.

James wasn't sure he believed he was an alien, but he also wasn't sure he disbelieved it.

He took a moment to drink in Shay's beauty, her

athletic body, her long dark hair, and even the brightness of her smile.

"Didn't you think I was gay?" James murmured.

Shay laughed. "We all make mistakes. I figured out that you're just thick. It's fine; I understand now. The question is, do you?" Her smile softened. "Do you understand how *I* feel?"

James stared into her eyes for a long while, not replying. "You sure about this? Especially after everything you've seen and found out about me? I'm not even human, according to you."

"Well, at least you have a human body."

James snorted. "Yeah, I do."

They stared at each other for another moment before they exited the pub hand in hand.

James put his fork and knife down, savoring the lingering flavor of the steak in his mouth. He looked at Shay and the smiling Alison.

"So yeah, it's all over, kid." He shot a glance at Shay. "Though I wish I had known earlier that Shay was giving you a play-by-play."

The tomb raider shrugged. "She deserves to know what's going on with her soon-to-be dad."

James grunted. "Yeah, well, Shay took out most of the assassins. I barely had to do sh...anything with them. The only one that gave us any trouble, Shay figured out how to weaken her, and when we were dealing with the Harriken she was a machine."

Alison fanned herself. "I believe I'm having a little girl crush on my awesome Aunt Shay."

A strange look passed over Shay's face and she shrugged.

Alison stood. "That said, I need to go to the bathroom. I'll be right back."

"Should I come with you?" Shay asked.

The teen shook her head. "I'm fine. I'll be right back." She waved and stood, carefully making her way toward the bathrooms.

James was awed by her ability to navigate without normal vision.

Shay sighed. "Damn it. I'm supposed to be showing her how to be a normal woman, not a killer."

James shrugged. "Just be you. Alison loves who you are, and she'll pick out the parts that work for her."

"Wow."

"What?"

"I'm shocked at the wisdom that just dropped out of the mouth of a rock."

James chuckled and picked up his fork and knife again. He wanted to down a few more pieces of juicy steak. It wasn't barbecue, but it was still damned good.

Might have to hit up yakiniku places more. That stuff really grew on me.

A few minutes later Alison returned and seated herself.

James swallowed a piece of meat and cleared his throat. "I need to be clear about something, Alison."

"What?"

"On whether you want me to adopt you or if you'd

rather just stay as my ward. I'll support you in whatever you want."

Alison frowned. "Why wouldn't I want you to adopt me?"

"I don't know. Your mom was special, and I'm...just me."

Shay snorted and rolled her eyes.

Yeah, well, she doesn't need to deal with the whole 'your new dad is an alien' thing yet, Shay. Alison's got enough on her plate.

Alison shook her head. "I've been learning about the Drow and it's been fascinating, but it doesn't matter that you're different than me because you're human."

Shay snorted again.

Alison shot her an annoyed look. "Anyway, like I said, it doesn't matter. Family is family, and I would love for you to adopt me. You're the first man who has actually cared for me, and it's funny how you pick on the boys."

"What boys?" James growled, looking around.

Shay and Alison shared a laugh.

After confirming there were no boys he needed to threaten in the vicinity, James returned his attention to Alison. "During your summer break, we can finish all your paperwork. We can also have a party, since the new house should be finished by then. You'll have your own bathroom and a huge closet; plenty of space."

Alison smiled and shrugged. "Thanks, but what do I need with all that space? What clothes am I going to put in it? What shoes?"

James sighed. He hated that she couldn't see everything. Her soul sight might give her a unique view of the world, but at the same time she was missing out on a lot of experiences.

The thought of giving her normal sight with the wish bubbled up, but he forced it back down. That wasn't his call to make, and now Alison knew about the wish. She could make that decision herself if she wanted. In time, she would figure out what was best for her—with his guidance.

"Don't worry about it," Alison told him. "I'm just happy I'm going to be your daughter officially." The girl let out a happy sigh. "I know you can't see it, but it's...beautiful how our energies are connected now."

James smiled. "That's great, kid. That's great."

"Oh, and does this mean Shay will be my mom?"

Shay spat out her water, her eyes wide.

James just laughed.

Guess I should have figured out she'd see that.

FINIS

Alison's journey continues in The School Of Necessary Magic. Book one in this new series, *Dark is Her Nature*, comes your way in June of 2018 exclusively at Amazon.

Available Now at Amazon

The man scratched his chin as he looked into the distance, thinking about my question. Brownstone turned to look back at me. "Just five minutes?"

"All I need," I agreed, touching the button on my iPhone to start the recording. "No barbeque this time, I promise."

Brownstone grunted, neither pleased nor displeased with my comment. That was the best result I could hope for, I figured. "Tell me about…"

"No Shay." He shook his head.

"I wasn't going to ask about Ms. Carson," I confirmed.

"No Alison," He added.

"I wasn't going to ask about Alison either," I admitted.

"Ok." He nodded. "If we aren't talking barbeque, Shay, or Alison, what is it you wish to chat about?"

"Trucks," I replied, and his face lit up a bit. Well, for Brownstone it damn near was as bright as the sun. "I'd like you to tell me what you think about the Hummer."

"Good," he admitted. "It held up when it got shot to shit

and took off-road efforts well." He smirked. "They cost a shitload when you total one." His eyes narrowed. "Wait, are you with the insurance company?"

"No." I sighed. "I've told you before, I'm The Author. I take your life and somewhat fictionalize it."

"Yeah." He shrugged. "But authors don't make any money."

"I'm fine," I answered.

"You sure?" He countered. "I could imagine you taking a second job to support your writing habit."

"It's not a *habit*." I pulled my phone out and clicked on the web browser. "Look! Have you ever paid any attention to my Author Page?"

"No," James answered. "Do you do barbeque books?"

I stopped typing into the search bar long enough to grunt and stare up at him from underneath my bushy eyebrows. "*No.*"

"Then no need to look you up," he finished.

This time I stayed quiet and turned my phone around, placing the book list (or at least the start of the book list) right in front of his face.

He didn't take the phone from my hand; his eyes merely went back and forth as he read.

"You can take it," I urged.

This wasn't some nice suggestion on my side. No, my fucking arm was getting tired after a few moments. I wanted him to *take the fucking phone*.

I type. *I don't work out.*

Finally he took the phone from my hand, swiping his finger across the screen and continuing to study the books there. "Thank you," I told him, massaging my arm where the muscles had started to cramp.

He grunted and I rolled my eyes. Why I ever chose to document his exploits is becoming fuzzier and fuzzier to me the more I interact with him. "You have pictures of Shay in here," he told me. I looked up to see him staring over the phone at me.

"Yes." I nodded. "She wanted the money for the stories."

"Sounds like Shay," he agreed and returned to looking at the screen. "You still sending the payments to the orphanage?"

"Yes." I nodded again. "Per our contract, I send it within five days of book income coming in. The first time the Father was quite surprised. I had to do a tap dance to make sure I answered his "is this money from blood business?" question correctly so he would accept the funds."

"What did you tell him?"

"That I was matching it from other books, not Shay's. He accepted the notion."

He handed me back my phone. "Lots of books," he admitted. "So, you don't have a second job?"

"No." I shook my head. "I'm a full-time writer making good money because the readers LOVE your stories."

"All right," He allowed.

"Ok, my question…"

He cut me off. "Out of time." He pointed to his watch with a smirk on his face.

I looked down and my shoulders drooped. It had been six minutes…

"Sonofabitch!"

That fucker is a lot smarter than we think he is.

Thank you for following us into this fourth story of James Brownstone! We have Shay #1 and #2 out, and will have Alison #1 Pre-Order on June 2nd (Pre-order, not the final release, which is June 6th.)

Right now life is crazy! I'm in Boston for the Boston Fantasy Fest and RIGHT after that I fly to New York for APAC and Book Expo (simultaneous event in New York.)

I'm ready to curl up into an introvert ball and hide.

I'm sure I'll do 'just fine' through the events, and be happy they happened, but hell's bells I'm kinda terrified of all the effort over the next eight days.

See you all on Social Media! (Sort of... Well, I'll post stuff, and you will see it... I don't think I'll actually *see* anyone.)

THANK YOU again for supporting this series, and all the other Oriceran books you have read.

We can't do what we do, without you!

Ad Aeternitatem,

Michael

Truth (3) - Land of Terran (4) - New Egypt (5) - Lancothy (6) - Virgo (7)

The Kacy Chronicles
* A.L. Knorr and Martha Carr *

Descendant (1) - Ascendant (2) - Combatant (3) - Transcendent (4)

The Midwest Magic Chronicles
* Flint Maxwell and Martha Carr*

The Midwest Witch (1) - The Midwest Wanderer (2) - The Midwest Whisperer (3) - The Midwest War (4)

The Fairhaven Chronicles
* with S.M. Boyce *

Glow (1) - Shimmer (2) - Ember (3) - Nightfall (4)

CONNECT WITH MICHAEL ANDERLE

Michael Anderle Social
   Website:
   http://kurtherianbooks.com/

Email List:
   http://kurtherianbooks.com/email-list/

Facebook Here:
   https://www.facebook.com/OriceranUniverse/
   https://www.facebook.com/TheKurtherianGambitBoo
ks/

Made in the USA
Middletown, DE
27 May 2019